# A LAND of FIRE

## (BOOK #12 IN THE SORCERER'S RING)

### MORGAN RICE

**Books by Morgan Rice**

# THE SORCERER'S RING
## A QUEST OF HEROES
## A MARCH OF KINGS
## A FEAST OF DRAGONS
## A CLASH OF HONOR
## A VOW OF GLORY
## A CHARGE OF VALOR
## A RITE OF SWORDS
## A GRANT OF ARMS
## A SKY OF SPELLS
## A SEA OF SHIELDS
## A REIGN OF STEEL
## A LAND OF FIRE

# THE SURVIVAL TRILOGY
## ARENA ONE (Book #1)
## ARENA TWO (Book #2)

# the Vampire Journals
## turned (book #1)
## loved (book #2)
## betrayed (book #3)
## destined (book #4)
## desired (book #5)
## betrothed (book #6)
## vowed (book #7)
## found (book #8)
## resurrected (book #9)
## craved (book #10)

"Thus I turn my back:
There is a world elsewhere."

--William Shakespeare
*Coriolanus*

# CHAPTER ONE

Gwendolyn stood on the shore of the Upper Isles, gazing out into the ocean, watching with horror as the fog rolled in and began to consume her baby. She felt as if her heart were breaking in two as she saw Guwayne floating farther and farther away, into the horizon, disappearing in the mist. The tide was carrying him God knows where, every second taking him more beyond her reach.

Tears rolled down Gwendolyn's cheeks as she watched, unable to tear herself away, numb to the world. She lost all sense of time and place, could no longer feel her body. A part of her died as she watched the person she loved most in the world be consumed by an ocean tide. It was as if a part of her were sucked out to sea with him.

Gwen hated herself for what she had done; yet at the same time, she knew it was the only thing in the world that might just save her child. Gwen heard the roaring and thundering on the horizon behind her, and she knew that soon, this entire island would be consumed with flame—and that nothing in the world could save them. Not Argon, who lay still in a helpless state; not Thorgrin, who was a world away, in the Land of the Druids; not Alistair or Erec, who were another world away, in the Southern Isles; and not Kendrick or the Silver or any of the other brave men who were here in this place, none of them with the means to combat a dragon. Magic was what they needed—and it was the one thing they had run out of.

They had been lucky to escape the Ring at all, and now, she knew, fate had caught up with them. There was no more running, no more hiding. It was time to face the death that had been chasing them.

Gwendolyn turned and faced the opposite horizon, and she could see even from here the black mass of dragons heading her way. She had little time; she did not want to die all alone here on these shores, but with her people, protecting them as best she could.

Gwen turned back for one last look out at the ocean, hoping for a last glimpse of Guwayne. But there was nothing. Guwayne was far from her now, somewhere on the horizon, already traveling to a world she would never know.

*Please, God*, Gwen prayed. *Be with him. Take my life for his. I will do anything. Keep Guwayne safe. Let me hold him again. I beg you. Please.*

Gwendolyn opened her eyes, hoping to see a sign, perhaps a rainbow in the sky—anything.

But the horizon was empty. There was nothing but black, glowering clouds, as if the universe were furious with her for what she had done.

Sobbing, Gwen turned her back on the ocean, on what remained of her life, and broke into a jog, each step taking her closer to make her final stand with her people.

\*

Gwen stood on the upper parapets of Tirus's fort, surrounded by dozens of her people, among them her brothers Kendrick and Reece and Godfrey, her cousins Matus and Stara, Steffen, Aberthol, Srog, Brandt, Atme, and all the Legion. They all faced the sky, silent and somber, knowing what was coming for them.

As they listened to the distant roars that shook the earth, they stood there, helpless, watching Ralibar wage their war for them, a single brave dragon fighting his best, holding off the host of enemy dragons. Gwen's heart soared as she watched Ralibar fight, so brave, so bold, one dragon against dozens and yet unafraid. Ralibar breathed fire on the dragons, raised his great talons and scratched them, clutched them, and sank his teeth into their throats. He was not only stronger than the others, but faster, too. He was a thing to watch.

As Gwen watched, her heart soared with its last ounce of hope; a part of her dared to believe that maybe Ralibar could defeat them. She saw Ralibar duck and dive down as three dragons breathed fire at his face, narrowly missing him. Ralibar then lunged forward and plunged his talons into one of the dragons' chest, and used his momentum to force it down toward the ocean.

Several dragons breathed fire onto Ralibar's back as he dove, and Gwen watched in horror as Ralibar and the other dragon became a flaming ball, dropping down to the sea. The dragon resisted, but Ralibar used all his weight to drive it down into the waves—and soon they both plunged into the ocean.

A great hissing noise arose, along with clouds of steam, as the water doused the fire. Gwen watched with anticipation, hoping he was okay—and moments later, Ralibar surfaced, alone. The other dragon surfaced too, but it was bobbing, floating on the waves, dead.

Without hesitating, Ralibar shot up toward the dozens of other dragons diving down at him. As they came down, their great jaws open, aiming for him, Ralibar was on the attack: he reached out his great talons, leaned back, spread his wings, and grabbed two of them, then spun around and drove them down into the sea.

Ralibar held them under, yet as he did, a dozen dragons pounced on Ralibar's exposed back. The whole group of them plummeted into the ocean, driving Ralibar down with them. Ralibar, as valiantly as he fought, was just way too outnumbered, and he plunged into the water, flailing, held down by dozens of dragons, screeching in fury.

Gwen swallowed, her heart breaking at the sight of Ralibar fighting for all of them, all alone out there; she wished more than anything that she could help him. She combed the surface of the ocean, waiting, hoping, for any sign of Ralibar, willing him to surface.

But to her horror, he never did.

The other dragons surfaced, and they all flew up, regrouped, and set their sights on the Upper Isles. They seemed to look right at Gwendolyn as they let out a great roar and spread their wings.

Gwen felt her heart splitting. Her dear friend Ralibar, their last hope, their last line of defense, was dead.

Gwen turned to her men, who stood staring in shock. They knew what was coming next: an unstoppable wave of destruction.

Gwen felt heavy; she opened her mouth, and the words stuck in her throat.

"Sound the bells," she finally said, her voice hoarse. "Command our people to shelter. Anyone above ground needs to go below, now. Into the caves, the cellars—anywhere but here. Command them—now!"

"Sound the bells!" Steffen yelled, running to the edge of the fort, screaming out over the courtyard. Soon, bells tolled throughout the square. Hundreds of her people, survivors from the Ring, now fled, racing to take shelter, heading for the caves on the outskirts of town or hurrying into cellars and shelters below ground, preparing themselves against the inevitable wave of fire that would come.

9

"My Queen," Srog said, turning to her, "perhaps we can all take shelter in this fort. After all, it is made of stone."

Gwen shook her head knowingly.

"You do not understand the dragons' wrath," she said. "Nothing above ground will be safe. Nothing."

"But my lady, perhaps we will be safer in this fort," he urged. "It has stood the test of time. These stone walls are a foot thick. Wouldn't you rather be here than underneath the earth?"

Gwen shook her head. There came a roar, and she looked to the horizon and could see the dragons approaching. Her heart broke as she saw, in the distance, the dragons breathing a wall of flame down onto her fleet that lay in the southern harbor. She watched as her precious ships, her lifeline off this island, beautiful ships that had taken decades to build, were reduced to nothing but kindling. She felt fortunate that she had anticipated this, and had hidden a few ships on the other side of the island. If they ever even survived to use them.

"There is no time for debate. All of us will leave this place at once. Follow me."

They followed Gwen as she hurried off the roof and down the spiral steps, taking them as fast as she could; as she went, Gwen instinctively reached out to clutch Guwayne—then her heart broke once again as she realized he was gone. She felt a part of her missing as she ran down the steps, hearing all the footsteps behind her, taking them two at a time, all of them rushing to get to safety. Gwen could hear the distant roars of the dragons getting closer, shaking the place already, and she only prayed that Guwayne was safe.

Gwen burst out of the castle and raced across the courtyard with the others, all of them running for the entrance to the dungeons, long emptied of prisoners. Several of her soldiers waited before the steel doors, opening up to steps leading down to the ground, and before they entered, Gwen stopped and turned to her people.

She saw several people still rushing about the courtyard, shrieking in fear, in a daze, unsure where to go.

"Come here!" she called out. "Come underground! All of you!"

Gwen stepped aside, making sure they all made it to safety first, and one by one, her people rushed past her, down the stone steps into the darkness.

The last people to stop and stand with her were her brothers, Kendrick and Reece and Godfrey, along with Steffen. The five of them turned and examined the sky together, as another earth-shattering roar came.

The host of dragons was now so close that Gwen could see them, hardly several hundred yards away, their great wings larger than life, all of them emboldened, faces filled with fury. Their great jaws were wide open, as if anticipating tearing them apart, and their teeth were each as large as Gwendolyn.

*So,* Gwendolyn thought, *this is what death looks like.*

Gwen took one last look around, and she saw hundreds of her people taking shelter in their new homes above ground, refusing to go below.

"I told them to get below ground!" Gwen yelled.

"Some of our people listened," Kendrick observed sadly, shaking his head, "but many would not."

Gwen felt herself breaking up inside. She knew what would happen to the people who stayed above ground. Why did her people always have to be so obstinate?

And then it happened—the first of the dragon fire came rolling toward them, far enough away so as not to burn them, yet close enough that Gwen could feel the heat scorching her face. She watched in horror as screams arose, coming from her people on the far side of the courtyard who had decided to wait above ground, inside their dwellings or inside Tirus's fort. The stone fort, so indomitable just moments before, was now ablaze, flames shooting out the sides and front and back, as if it were nothing but a house of flame, its stone charred and seared in but a moment. Gwen swallowed hard, knowing that if they had tried to wait it out in the fort, they would all be dead.

Others had not been so lucky: they shrieked, ablaze, and ran through the streets before collapsing to the earth. The horrible smell of burning flesh cut through the air.

"My lady," Steffen said, "we must go below. Now!"

Gwen could not bear to tear herself away, and yet she knew he was right. She allowed herself to be led by the others, to be dragged down through the gates, down the steps, into the blackness, as a wave of flame came rolling toward her. The steel doors slammed closed a second before they reached her, and as she heard them reverberate behind her, they felt like a door slamming closed in her heart.

# CHAPTER TWO

Alistair, sobbing, knelt beside Erec's body, clutching him tight, her wedding dress covered in his blood. As she held him, her entire world spinning, she felt the life flow beginning to ebb out of him. Erec, riddled with stab wounds, was moaning, and she could sense by the rhythms of his pulse that he was dying.

"NO!" Alistair moaned, cradling him in her arms, rocking him. She felt her heart rend in two as she held him, felt as if she were dying herself. This man whom she had been about to marry, who had looked at her with such love just moments before, now lay nearly lifeless in her arms; she could hardly process it. He had received the blow so unsuspecting, so filled with love and joy; he had been caught off guard because of her. Because of her stupid game, asking him to close his eyes while she approached with her dress. Alistair felt overwhelmed with guilt, as if it were all her fault.

"Alistair," he moaned.

She looked down and saw his eyes half open, saw them becoming dull, the life force beginning to leave them.

"Know that this is not your fault," he whispered. "And know how much I love you."

Alistair wept, holding him to her chest, feeling him growing cold. As she did, something inside her snapped, something that felt the injustice of it all, something that absolutely refused to allow him to die.

Alistair suddenly felt a familiar, tingly feeling, like a thousand pinpricks in the tips of her fingers, and she felt her entire body flush with heat from head to toe. A strange force overtook her, something strong and primal, something she did not understand; it came on stronger than any surge of force she had ever felt in her life, like an outside spirit taking over her body. She felt her hands and arms burning hot, and she reflexively reached out and placed her palms on Erec's chest and forehead.

Alistair held them there, her hands burning ever hotter, and she closed her eyes. Images flashed through her mind. She saw Erec as a youth, leaving the Southern Isles, so proud and noble, standing on a tall ship; she saw him entering the Legion; joining the Silver; jousting, becoming a champion, defeating enemies, defending the Ring. She saw him sitting erect, posture perfect on his horse, in shining silver, a model of nobility and courage. She knew she could not let him die; the world could not afford to let him die.

Alistair's hands grew hotter still, and she opened her eyes and saw his eyes closing. She also saw a white light emanating from her palms, spreading all over Erec; she saw him infused with it, surrounded by a globe. And as she watched, she saw his wounds, seeping blood, slowly begin to seal up.

Erec's eyes flashed open, filled with light, and she felt something shift within him. His body, so cold just moments before, began to warm. She felt his life force returning.

Erec looked up at her in surprise and wonder, and as he did, Alistair felt her own energy depleted, her own life force lessening, as she transferred her energy to him.

His eyes closed and he fell into a deep sleep. Her hands suddenly grew cool, and she checked his pulse, felt it return to normal.

She sighed with great relief, knowing she had brought him back. Her palms shook, so drained from the experience, and she felt depleted, yet elated.

*Thank you, God*, she thought, as she leaned down, laid her face on his chest, and hugged him with tears of joy. *Thank you for not taking my husband from me.*

Alistair stopped crying, and she looked over and took in the scene: she saw Bowyer's sword lying there on the stone, its hilt and blade covered in blood. She hated Bowyer with a passion more than she could conceive; she was determined to avenge Erec.

Alistair reached down and picked up the bloody sword; her palms were covered in blood as she held it up, examining it. She prepared to cast it away, to watch it go clattering to the far end of the room— when suddenly, the door to the room burst open.

Alistair turned, the bloody sword in hand, to see Erec's family rush into the room, flanked by a dozen soldiers. As they came closer, their expressions of alarm turned to one of horror, as they all looked from her to the unconscious Erec.

"What have you done?" Dauphine cried out.

Alistair looked back at her, uncomprehending.

"I?" she asked. "I have done nothing."

Dauphine glowered as she stormed closer.

"Have you?" she said. "You've only killed our best and greatest knight!"

Alistair stared back at her in horror as she suddenly realized they were all looking at her as if she were a murderer.

She looked down and saw the bloody sword in her hand, saw the bloodstains on her palm and all over her dress, and she realized they all thought she had done it.

"But I did not stab him!" Alistair protested.

"No?" Dauphine accused. "Then did the sword appear magically in your hand?"

Alistair looked about the room, as they all gathered around her.

"It was a man who did this. The man who challenged him on the field in battle: Bowyer."

The others looked to each other, skeptical.

"Oh was it, then?" Dauphine countered. "And where is this man?" she asked, looking all about the room.

Alistair saw no sign of him, and she realized they all thought she was lying.

"He fled," she said. "After he stabbed him."

"And then how did his bloody sword get into your hand?" Dauphine countered.

Alistair looked down at the sword in her hand in horror, and she flung it, clanging across the stone.

"But why would I kill my own husband-to-be?" she asked.

"You are a sorcerer," Dauphine said, standing over her now. "Your kind are not to be trusted. Oh, my brother!" Dauphine said, rushing forward, dropping down to her knees beside Erec, getting between him and Alistair. Dauphine hugged Erec, clutching him.

"What have you done?" Dauphine moaned, between tears.

"But I am innocent!" Alistair exclaimed.

Dauphine turned to her with an expression of hatred, and then turned to all the soldiers.

"Arrest her!" she commanded.

Alistair felt hands grabbing her from behind, as she was yanked to her feet. Her energy was depleted, and she was unable to resist as the guards bound her wrists behind her back and began to drag her away. She cared little for what happened to her—yet, as they dragged her away, she could not bear the thought of being apart from Erec. Not now, not when he needed her most. The healing she had given him was only temporary; she knew that he needed another session, and that if he did not get it, he would die.

"NO!" she yelled. "Let me go!"

But her shouts fell on deaf ears as they dragged her away, shackled, as if she were just another common prisoner.

# CHAPTER THREE

Thor raised his hands to his eyes, blinded by the light, as the shining, golden doors to his mother's castle opened wide, so intense he could barely see. A figure walked out toward him, a silhouette, a woman he sensed, in every fiber of his being, to be his mother. Thor's heart pounded as he saw her standing there, arms at her side, facing him.

Slowly, the light began to fade, just enough for him to lower his hands and look at her. It was the moment he had been waiting for his entire life, the moment that had haunted him in his dreams. He could not believe it: it was really her. His mother. Inside this castle, perched atop this cliff. Thor opened his eyes fully and laid eyes upon her for the first time, standing but a few feet away, staring back. For the first time, he saw her face.

Thor's breath caught in his throat as he looked back at the most beautiful woman he had ever seen. She looked timeless, at once both old and young, her skin nearly translucent, her face shining. She smiled back at him sweetly, her long blonde hair falling down past her stomach, her big bright translucent gray eyes, her perfectly chiseled cheekbone and jawline matching his. What surprised Thor most as he stared at her was that he could recognize many of his own features in her face—the curve of her jaw, her lips, the shade of her gray eyes, even her proud forehead. In some ways, it was like staring back at himself. She also looked strikingly like Alistair.

Thor's mother, dressed in a white silk robe and cloak, the hood pulled back, stood with her palms out to her sides, adorned with no jewelry, her palms smooth, her skin like that of a baby's. Thor could feel the intense energy exuding from her, more intense than he had ever felt, like the sun, enveloping him. As he stood basking in it, he felt waves of love directed toward him. He had never before felt such unconditional love and acceptance. He felt like he *belonged*.

Standing here now, before her, Thor finally felt as if a part of him were complete, as if all was okay in the world.

"Thorgrin, my son," she said.

It was the most beautiful voice he'd ever heard, soft, reverberating off the ancient stone walls of the castle, sounding as if it had come down from heaven itself. Thor stood there in shock, not knowing what to do or what to say. Was this all real? He wondered briefly if it was all just another creation in the Land of the Druids, just another dream, or his mind playing tricks on him. He had been wanting to embrace his mother for as long as he could remember, and he took a step forward, determined to know if she was an apparition.

Thor reached out to embrace her, and as he did, he was afraid that his hug would go through nothing but air, all of this just an illusion. But as Thor reached out, he felt his arms wrap around her, felt himself hug a real person—and he felt her hug him back. It was the most amazing feeling in the world.

She hugged him tight, and Thor was elated to know that she was real. That this was all real. That he had a mother, that she really existed, that she was here in the flesh, in this land of illusion and fantasy—and that she really cared about him.

After a long while, they leaned back, and Thor looked at her, tears in his eyes, and saw that there were tears in hers, too.

"I'm so proud of you, my son," she said.

He stared back, at a loss for words.

"You have completed your journey," she added. "You are worthy to be here. You have become the man I always knew you would."

Thor looked back at her, taking in her features, still amazed by the fact that she really existed, and wondering what to say. His entire life he'd had so many questions for her; yet now that he was here before her, he was drawing a blank. He wasn't sure even where to begin.

"Come with me," she said, turning, "and I will show you this place—this place where you were born."

She smiled and held out her hand, and Thor grasped it.

They walked side-by-side into the castle, his mother leading the way, light exuding off of her and bouncing off the walls. Thor took it all in in wonder: it was the most resplendent place he'd ever seen, its walls made of sparkling gold, everything shining, perfect, surreal. He felt as if he had come to a magical castle in heaven.

They passed down a long corridor with high arched ceilings, light bouncing off of everything. Thor looked down and saw the floor was covered in diamonds, smooth, sparkling in a million points of light.

"Why did you leave me?" Thor suddenly asked.

They were the first words Thor had spoken, and they surprised even him. Of all the things he wanted to ask her, for some reason this popped out first, and he felt embarrassed and ashamed that he hadn't anything nicer to say. He hadn't meant to be so abrupt.

But his mother's compassionate smile never faltered. She walked beside him, looking at him with pure love, and he could feel such love and acceptance from her, could feel that she did not judge him, no matter what he said.

"You are right to be upset with me," she said. "I need to ask your forgiveness. You and your sister meant more to me than anything in the world. I wanted to raise you here—but I could not. Because you are both special. Both of you."

They turned down another corridor, and his mother stopped and turned to Thor.

"You are not just a Druid, Thorgrin, not just a warrior. You are the greatest warrior that has ever been, or ever will be—and the greatest Druid, too. Yours is a special destiny; your life is meant to be bigger, much bigger, than this place. It is life and a destiny meant to be shared with the world. That is why I set you free. I had to let you out in the world, in order for you to become the man you are, in order for you to have the experiences you had and to learn to become the warrior you are meant to be."

She took a deep breath.

"You see, Thorgrin, it is not seclusion and privilege that make a warrior—but toil and hardship, suffering and pain. Suffering above all. It killed me to watch you suffer—and yet paradoxically, that was what you needed most in order to become the man you have become. Do you understand, Thorgrin?"

Thor did indeed, for the first time in his life, understand. For the first time, it all made sense. He thought of all the suffering he had encountered in his life: his being raised without a mother, reared as a lackey to his brothers, by a father who hated him, in a small, suffocating village, viewed by everyone as a nobody. His upbringing had been one long string of indignities.

But now he was beginning to see that he needed that; that all of his toil and tribulation was meant to be.

"All of your hardship, your independence, your struggling to find your own way," his mother added, "it was my gift to you. It was my gift to make you stronger."

*A gift*, Thorgrin thought to himself. He had never thought of it that way before. At the time, it felt like the farthest thing from a gift— yet now, looking back, he knew that it was exactly that. As she spoke the words, he realized that she was right. All the adversity in his life that he had faced—it had all been a gift, to help mold him into what he had become.

His mother turned, and the two continued to walk side-by-side through the castle, and Thor's mind spun with a million questions for her.

"Are you real?" Thor asked.

Once again, he was ashamed for being so blunt, and once again he found himself asking a question he did not expect to ask. Yet he felt an intense desire to know.

"Is this place real?" Thor added. "Or is it all just illusion, just a figment of my own imagination, like the rest of this land?"

His mother smiled at him.

"I am as real as you," she replied.

Thor nodded, assured at the response.

"You are correct that the Land of Druids is a land of illusion, a magic land within yourself," she added. "I am very much real—yet at the same time, like you, I am a Druid. Druids are not so attached to physical place as are humans. Which means that a part of me lives here, while a part of me lives elsewhere. That is why I am always with you, even if you cannot see me. Druids are everywhere and nowhere at once. We straddle two worlds that others do not."

"Like Argon," Thor replied, recalling Argon's distant gaze, his sometimes appearing and disappearing, his being everywhere and nowhere at once.

She nodded.

"Yes," she replied. "Just like my brother."

Thor gaped, in shock.

"Your brother?" he repeated.

She nodded.

20

"Argon is your uncle," she said. "He loves you very much. He always has. And Alistair, too."

Thor pondered it all, overwhelmed.

His brow furrowed as he thought of something.

"But for me, it's different," Thor said. "I don't quite feel as you. I feel more of an attachment to place than you. I can't travel to other worlds as freely as Argon."

"That is because you are half human," she replied.

Thor thought about that.

"I am here now, in this castle, in my home," he said. "This is my home, is it not?"

"Yes," she replied. "It is. Your true home. As much as any home you have in the world. Yet Druids are not as attached to the concept of home."

"So if I wanted to stay here, to live here, I could?" Thor asked.

His mother shook her head.

"No," she said. "Because your time here, in the Land of the Druids, is finite. Your arriving here was destined—yet you can only visit the Land of the Druids once. When you leave, you can never return again. This place, this castle, everything you see and know here, this place of your dreams that you have seen for so many years, it will all be gone. Like a river that cannot be stepped in twice."

"And you?" Thor asked, suddenly afraid.

His mother shook her head sweetly.

"You shall not see me again, either. Not like this. Yet I will always be with you."

Thor was crestfallen at the thought.

"But I don't understand," Thor said. "I finally found you. I finally found this place, my home. And now you are telling me it is just for this once?"

His mother sighed.

"A warrior's home is out in the world," she said. "It is your duty to be out there, to assist others, to defend others—and to be become, always, a better warrior. You can always become better. Warriors are not meant to sit in one place—especially not a warrior with a great destiny such as yours. You will encounter great things in your life: great castles, great cities, great peoples. Yet you must not cling to anything. Life is a great tide, and you must allow it to take you where it will."

Thor furrowed his brow, trying to understand. It was so much to take in at once.

"I always thought that, once I found you, my greatest quest would be finished."

She smiled back at him.

"That is the nature of life," she replied. "We are given great quests, or we choose them for ourselves, and we set out to achieve them. We never truly imagine we can achieve them—and yet, somehow, we do. Once we do, once one quest is complete, somehow we expect our lives to be over. But our lives are just beginning. Climbing one peak is a great accomplishment in itself—yet it also leads to another, greater, peak. Achieving one quest enables you to embark on another, greater, quest."

Thor looked at her, surprised.

"That's right," she said, reading his mind. "Your finding me will lead you now to another—greater—quest."

"What other quest can there be?" Thor asked. "What can be greater than finding you?"

She smiled back, her eyes filled with wisdom.

"You cannot even begin to imagine the quests that lay ahead of you," she said. "Some people in life are born with just one quest. Some people, none. But you—Thorgrin—have been born with a destiny of twelve quests."

"Twelve?" Thor repeated, flabbergasted.

She nodded.

"The Destiny Sword was one. You achieved that marvelously. Finding me was another. You have achieved two of them. You have ten more to go, ten quests even greater than those two."

"Ten more?" he asked. "Greater? How is it possible?"

"Let me show you," she said, as she came up beside him and draped an arm around him and led him gently down the corridor. She led him through a shining sapphire door, and into a room made entirely of sapphires, sparkling green.

Thor's mother led him across the room to a huge, arched window made of crystal. Thor stood beside her and reached up and placed a palm on the crystal, sensing he needed to, and as he did, the two windowpanes gently opened.

Thor looked out at the ocean, a sweeping panorama from here, covered in a blinding haze and fog, a white light bouncing off of everything, making it seem as if they were perched atop heaven itself.

"Look out," she said. "Tell me what you see."

Thor looked out, and at first he saw nothing but ocean and white haze. Soon, though, the haze turned brighter, the ocean began to disappear, and images began to flash before him.

The first thing Thor saw was his son, Guwayne, out at sea, floating on a small boat.

Thor's heart raced in panic.

"Guwayne," he said. "Is it true?"

"Even now he is lost at sea," she said. "He needs you. Finding him will be one of the great quests of your life."

As Thor watched Guwayne floating away, he felt an urgency to leave this place at once, to race to the ocean.

"I must go to him—now!"

His mother laid a calming hand on his wrist.

"See what else you have to see," she said.

Thor looked out and saw Gwendolyn and her people; they sat huddled on a rocky island and braced themselves as a wall of dragons descended from the sky, blanketing them. He saw a wall of flame, bodies on fire, people screaming in agony.

Thor's heart pounded with urgency.

"Gwendolyn," Thor cried. "I must go to her."

His mother nodded.

"She needs you, Thorgrin. They all need you—and they also need a new home."

As Thor continued to watch, he saw the landscape transform, and he saw the entire Ring devastated, a blackened landscape, Romulus's million men covering every inch of it.

"The Ring," he said, horrified. "It is no more."

Thor felt a burning desire to race from here and rescue them all right now.

His mother reached out and closed the window panes, and he turned and faced her.

"Those are just some of the quests that lay before you," she said. "Your child needs you, Gwendolyn needs you, your people need you—and beyond that, you will need to prepare for the day when you shall become King."

Thor's eyes opened wide.

"I? King?"

His mother nodded.

"It is your destiny, Thorgrin. You are the last hope. It is you who must become King of the Druids."

"King of the Druids?" he asked, trying to comprehend. "But...I don't understand. I thought I was in the Land of the Druids."

"The Druids do not live here anymore," his mother explained. "We are a nation in exile. They live now in a distant kingdom, in the far reaches of the Empire, and they are in great danger. You are destined to become their King. They need you, and you need them. Collectively, your power will be needed to battle the greatest power ever known to us. A threat far greater than the dragons."

Thor stared back, wondering.

"I'm so confused, Mother," he admitted.

"That is because your training is incomplete. You have advanced greatly, but you haven't even begun to reach the levels you will need to become a great warrior. You will meet powerful new teachers who will guide you, who will bring you to levels higher than you can imagine. You haven't even begun to see the warrior you will become.

"And you will need it, all of their training," she continued. "You will face monstrous empires, kingdoms greater than anything you've ever seen. You will encounter savage tyrants that make Andronicus look like nothing."

His mother examined him, her eyes full of knowing and compassion.

"Life is always bigger than you imagine, Thorgrin," she continued. "Always bigger. The Ring, in your eyes, is a great kingdom, the center of the world. But it is a small kingdom compared to the rest of the world; it is but a speck in the Empire. There are worlds, Thorgrin, beyond what you can imagine, bigger than anything you've seen. You have not even begun to live." She paused. "You will need this."

Thor looked down as he felt something on his wrist, and he watched as his mother clasped a bracelet on it, several inches wide, covering half of his forearm. It was shining gold, with a single black diamond in its center. It was the most beautiful, and the most powerful, thing he'd ever seen, and as it sat on his wrist, he felt its power throbbing, infusing him.

"As long as you wear this," she said, "no man born of woman can harm you."

Thor looked back at her, and in his mind flashed the images he'd seen beyond those crystal windows, and he felt anew the urgency to Guwayne, to save Gwendolyn, to save his people.

But a part of him did not want to leave here, this place of his dreams to which he could never return, did not want to leave his mother.

He examined his bracelet, feeling the power of it overwhelming him. He felt as if it carried a piece of his mother.

"Is that why we were meant to meet?" Thor asked. "So that I could receive this?"

She nodded.

"And more importantly," she said, "to receive my love. As a warrior, you must learn to hate. But equally important, you must learn to love. Love is the stronger of the two forces. Hatred can kill a man, but love can raise him up, and it takes more power to heal than it does to kill. You must know hate, but you must also know love—and you must know when to choose each. You must learn not only to love, but more importantly, to allow yourself to receive love. Just as we need meals, we need love. You must know how much I love you. How much I accept you. How proud of you I am. You must know that I am always with you. And you must know that we will meet again. In the meantime, allow my love to carry you through. And more importantly, allow yourself to love and accept yourself."

Thor's mother stepped forward and hugged him, and he hugged her back. It felt so good to hold her, to know he had a mother, a real mother, who existed in the world. As he held her, he felt himself filling up with love, and it made him feel sustained, born anew, ready to face anything.

Thor leaned back and looked into her eyes. They were his eyes, gray eyes, gleaming.

She lay both palms on his head, leaned forward, and kissed his forehead. Thor closed his eyes, and he never wanted the moment to end.

Thor suddenly felt a cool breeze on his arms, heard the sound of crashing waves, felt moist ocean air. He opened his eyes and looked about in surprise.

To his shock, his mother was gone. Her castle was gone. The cliff was gone. He looked all around, and he saw that he stood on a beach, the scarlet beach that lay at the entrance to the Land of the Druids. He had somehow exited the Land of the Druids. And he was all alone.

His mother had vanished.

Thor looked down at his wrist, at his new golden bracelet with the black diamond in its center, and he felt transformed. He felt his mother with him, felt her love, felt able to conquer the world. He felt stronger than he ever had. He felt ready to head into battle against any foe, to save his wife, his child.

Hearing a purring sound, Thor looked over and was elated to see Mycoples sitting not far away, slowly lifting her great wings. She purred and walked toward him, and Thor felt that Mycoples was ready, too.

As she approached, Thor looked down and was shocked to see something sitting on the beach, which had been hidden beneath her. It was white, large, and round. Thor looked closely and saw that it was an egg.

A dragon's egg.

Mycoples looked to Thor, and Thor looked at her, shocked. Mycoples looked back at the egg sadly, as if not wanting to leave it but knowing that she had to. Thor stared at the egg in wonder, and he wondered what sort of dragon would emerge from Mycoples and Ralibar. He felt it would be the greatest dragon known to man.

Thor mounted Mycoples, and the two of them turned and took one long last look at the Land of the Druids, this mysterious place that had welcomed Thor in, and thrown him out. It was a place Thor was in awe of, a place he would never quite understand.

Thor turned and looked at the great ocean before them.

"It is time for war, my friend," Thor commanded, his voice booming, confident, the voice of a man, of a warrior, of a King-to-be.

Mycoples screeched, raised her great wings, and lifted the two of them up into the sky, over the ocean, away from this world, heading back for Guwayne, for Gwendolyn, for Romulus, his dragons, and the battle of Thor's life.

# CHAPTER FOUR

Romulus stood at the bow of his ship, first in the fleet, thousands of Empire ships behind him, and he looked out at the horizon with great satisfaction. High overhead flew his host of dragons, their screeches filling the air, battling Ralibar. Romulus clutched the railing as he watched, digging his long fingernails into it, gripping the wood as he watched his beasts attack Ralibar and drive him down into the ocean, again and again, pinning him beneath the waters.

Romulus cried out in joy and squeezed the rail so hard that it shattered as he watched his dragons shoot up from the ocean, victorious, with no sign of Ralibar. Romulus raised his hands high above his head and leaned forward, feeling a power burning in his palms.

"Go, my dragons," he whispered, eyes aglow. "Go."

No sooner had he uttered the words than his dragons turned and set their sights on the Upper Isles; they raced forward, screeching, raising their wings high. Romulus could feel himself controlling them, could feel himself invincible, able to control anything in the universe. After all, it was still his moon. His time of power would be up soon, but for now, nothing in the world could stop him.

Romulus's eyes lit up as he watched the dragons aim for the Upper Isles, saw in the distance men and women and children running and screaming from their path. He watched with delight as the flames began to roll down, as people were burned alive, and as the entire island went up in one huge ball of flame and destruction. He savored watching it be destroyed, just the same way he had watched the Ring destroyed.

Gwendolyn had managed to run from him—but this time, there was nowhere left to go. Finally, the last of the MacGils would be crushed under his hand forever. Finally, there would be no corner left of the universe that was not subjugated to him.

Romulus turned and looked over his shoulder at his thousands of ships, his immense fleet filling the horizon, and he breathed deep and leaned back, raising his face to the heavens, raising his palms up to his sides, and he shrieked a shriek of victory.

# CHAPTER FIVE

Gwendolyn stood in the cavernous stone cellar underground, huddled with dozens of her people, and listened to the earth quake and burn above her. Her body flinched with every noise. The earth shook hard enough at times to make them stumble and fall, as outside, huge chunks of rubble smashed to the ground, the playthings of the dragons. The sound of it rumbling and reverberating echoed endlessly in Gwen's ears, sounding as if the whole world were being destroyed.

The heat became more and more intense below ground as the dragons breathed down on the steel doors above, again and again, as if knowing they were hiding under here. The flames luckily were stopped by the steel, yet black smoke seeped through, making it ever harder to breathe, and sending them all into coughing fits.

There came the awful sound of stone smashing against steel, and Gwen watched as the steel doors above her bent and shook, and nearly caved in. Clearly, the dragons knew they were down here, and were trying their best to get in.

"How long will the gates hold?" Gwen asked Matus, standing close by.

"I do not know," Matus replied. "My father built this underground cellar to withstand attack from enemies—not from dragons. I do not think it can last very long."

Gwendolyn felt death closing in on her as the room became hotter and hotter, feeling as if she were standing on a scorched earth. It became harder to see from the smoke, and the floor trembled as rubble smashed again and again above them, small pieces of rock and dust crumbling down onto her head.

Gwen looked around at the terrified faces of all those in the room, and she could not help but wonder if, by retreating down here, they had all set themselves up for a slow and painful death. She was starting to wonder if perhaps the people who had died up above, right away, were the lucky ones.

Suddenly there came a reprieve, as the dragons flew off elsewhere. Gwen was surprised, and wondered what they were up to, when moments later, she heard a tremendous crash of rock and the earth shook so strongly that everyone in the room fell. The crash had been distant, and was followed by two trembles, like a landslide of rock.

"Tirus's fort," Kendrick said, coming up beside her. "They must have destroyed it."

Gwen looked up at the ceiling and realized he was probably right. What else could elicit such an avalanche of rock? Clearly, the dragons were in a rage, intent on destroying every last thing on this isle. She knew it would only be a matter of time until they burst through to this chamber, too.

In the sudden lull, Gwen was shocked to hear the shrill sound of a baby's cry cutting through the air. The sound pierced her like a knife in her chest. She could not help but immediately think of Guwayne, and as the cry, somewhere above ground, grew louder, a part of her, still distraught, convinced herself that it was indeed Guwayne up there, crying out for her. She knew rationally that it was impossible; her son was out on the ocean, far from here. And yet, her heart begged for it to be so.

"My baby!" Gwen screamed. "He's up there. I must save him!"

Gwen ran for the steps, when suddenly she felt a strong hand on hers.

She turned to see her brother Reece holding her back.

"My lady," he said. "Guwayne is far from here. That is the cry of another baby."

Gwen did not wish it to be true.

"It is still a baby," she said. "It is all alone up there. I cannot let it die."

"If you go up there," Kendrick said, stepping forward, coughing in the soot, "we will have to close the doors after you, and you will be all alone up there. You will die up there."

Gwen was not thinking clearly. In her mind, there was a baby alive up there, all alone, and she knew, above all, that she had to save it—no matter what the price.

Gwen shook her hand free from Reece's grip and sprinted for the stairs. She took them three at a time, and before anyone could reach her, she pulled back the metal pole barring the doors, and leaned into

31

them with her shoulder, pushing them up with all her might as she raised her palms.

Gwen screamed out in pain as she did, the metal so hot it burned her palms, and quickly she retracted them; undeterred, she then covered her palms with her sleeves and pushed the doors up all the way.

Gwendolyn coughed madly as she burst out into daylight, clouds of black smoke pouring out of the underground with her. As she stumbled to the surface, she squinted against the light, then looked out, raising a hand to her eyes, and was shocked to see one huge wave of destruction. All that had been standing just moments before was now razed, reduced to piles of smoking and charred rubble.

The baby's cries came again, louder up here, and Gwen looked around, waiting for the black clouds of smoke to part; as she did, she saw, on the far side of the court, a baby on the ground, wrapped in a blanket. Nearby, she saw its parents lying, burnt alive, now dead. Somehow, the baby had survived. Perhaps, Gwen thought with a pang of misery, the mother had died sheltering it from the flames.

Suddenly, Kendrick, Reece, Godfrey, and Steffen appeared beside her.

"My lady, you must come back now!" Steffen implored. "You shall die up here!"

"The baby," Gwen said. "I must save it."

"You cannot," Godfrey insisted. "You will never make it back alive!"

Gwen no longer cared. Her mind was overcome with a laser-like focus, and all she saw, all she could think of, was the child. She blocked out the rest of the world and knew that, as much as she needed to breathe, she needed to save it.

The others tried to grab her, but Gwen was undeterred; she shook off their grip and dashed for the baby.

Gwen sprinted with all she had, heart slamming in her chest as she ran through the rubble, through clouds of billowing black smoke, flames all around her. The black smoke acted as a shield, though, and luckily for her, the dragons could not see her yet. She ran across the courtyard, through the clouds, seeing only the baby, hearing only its cries.

She ran and ran, her lungs bursting, until she finally reached it. She reached down and scooped up the baby and immediately examined its face, some part of her expecting to see Guwayne.

She was crestfallen to see it was not him; it was a girl. She had large, beautiful blue eyes filled with tears as she shrieked and trembled, her hands in fists. Still, Gwen felt elated to hold another baby, feeling as if somehow she were making amends for sending Guwayne away. And she could already see, after a brief glance at the baby's sparkling eyes, that it was beautiful.

The clouds of smoke lifted and Gwendolyn suddenly found herself exposed at the far end of the courtyard, holding the wailing baby. She looked up and saw, hardly a hundred yards away, a dozen fierce dragons, with huge glowing eyes, all turning and looking at her. They fixed their eyes on her with delight and fury, and she could see that they were already preparing to kill her.

The dragons launched into the air, flapping their great wings, so enormous from this close, heading her way. Gwen braced herself, standing there, clutching the baby, knowing she would never make it back in time.

Suddenly, there came the sound of drawn swords, and Gwen turned to see her brothers Reece, Kendrick, and Godfrey, along with Steffen, Brandt, Atme, and all the Legion members, standing beside her, all drawing swords and shields, all rushing to protect her. They formed a circle around her, holding their shields up to the sky, and they all prepared to die with her. Gwen was so deeply moved and inspired by their courage.

The dragons bore down on them, opening their massive jaws, and they braced themselves for the inevitable flame that would kill them all. Gwen closed her eyes and she saw her father, saw everyone who was ever important in her life, and she prepared to meet them.

Suddenly, there came a horrific shriek, and Gwen flinched, assuming it was the first attack.

But then she realized it was a different screech, one she recognized: the screech of an old friend.

Gwen looked up to the skies behind her, and she was overcome as she spotted a lone dragon racing through the skies, hurrying to do battle with the ones approaching her. She was even more elated to see, on its back, the man she loved more than anyone in the world:

Thorgrin.
He had returned.

# CHAPTER SIX

Thor rode on the back of Mycoples, the clouds whipping his face, going so fast he could hardly breathe, as they raced for the host of dragons and prepared for battle. Thor's bracelet throbbed on his wrist, and he felt that his mother had infused him with a new power which he could hardly understand; it was as if there were little sense of space and time. Thor had barely thought of flying back, had barely lifted from the shores of the Land of the Druids, when he was suddenly here already, above the Upper Isles, racing into the nest of dragons. Thor felt as if he had been magically transported here, as though they had traveled through a gap in time or space—as if his mother had launched them here, had somehow allowed them to achieve the impossible, to fly faster and farther than he ever had before. He felt it was his mother sending him off with a gift of speed.

As Thor squinted through the cloud cover, the immense dragons came into view, circling the Upper Isles, diving down and preparing to breathe fire. Thor looked down and his heart dropped to see that the island was already engulfed in flame, razed to the ground. He wondered with dread if anyone had managed to survive; he did not see how they could have. Was he too late?

Yet as Mycoples dove down, came ever closer, Thor's eyes narrowed in on a single person, drawing him in like a magnet as he singled her out in the chaos: Gwendolyn.

There she was, his wife-to-be, standing in the courtyard proudly, fearlessly, clutching a baby, surrounded by everyone Thor loved, all of them encircling her and raising shields to the sky as the dragons dove down to attack. Thor watched in horror as the dragons opened their great jaws and prepared to breathe flames that Thor knew, in but a moment, would consume Gwendolyn and everyone he loved.

"DIVE!" Thor screamed to Mycoples.

Mycoples needed no encouragement: she dove down faster than Thor could imagine, so fast he could hardly catch his breath, and he held on for dear life as she did, nearly upside down. Within moments she reached the three dragons about to attack Gwendolyn, and with a great roar, her jaw opened wide, her talons out before her, Mycoples attacked the unsuspecting beasts.

Mycoples smashed into the dragons, her downward momentum carrying her, landing on their backs, clawing one and biting another—and swiping the third with her wings. She stopped them right before they breathed fire, driving them face-first into the earth.

They all impacted the ground together, and there came a great rumble and clouds of dust as Mycoples drove their faces down beneath the earth, until they were lodged so deeply in it that they were stuck, only their rear talons sticking up out of the ground. As they touched down, Thor turned and saw Gwendolyn's shocked expression, and he thanked God that he'd saved her just in time.

There came a great roar, and Thor turned and looked back up to the sky, and faced an onslaught of approaching dragons.

Mycoples was already turning and flying upwards, launching, heading up for the dragons fearlessly. Thor was weaponless, but he felt different than he ever had entering a battle: for the first time in his life, he felt he did not need weapons. He felt he could summon and rely on the power within him. His true power. The power his mother had instilled him with.

As they approached, Thor held up his wrist, aiming his golden bracelet, and a light shot forth from the black diamond in its center. The yellow light engulfed the dragon closest to them, in the center of the pack, and knocked him backwards, sending him racing through the air, upwards, colliding into the others.

Mycoples, in a rage, determined to wreak havoc, dove fearlessly into the nest of dragons, fighting and clawing her way through, sinking her teeth into one, throwing another, and cutting a path through them as she knocked several of them back. She clamped down on one until it went limp and then dropped it; it fell to earth like a huge boulder falling from the sky, and hit the ground, shaking it. Thor could hear the impact from here as it caused another earthquake down below.

Thor glanced down below and saw Gwen and the others running to take cover, and he knew that he needed to direct all these dragons away from the island, away from Gwendolyn, in order to give them a chance to escape. If he led the dragons out to the ocean, he figured he could lure them away and take the fight out there.

"To the open sea!" Thor cried.

Mycoples followed his command, and they turned and flew through the nest of dragons and out the other side.

Thor turned as he heard a roar, and felt a distant heat as flames launched his way. He was satisfied to see his plan was working: all the dragons had abandoned the Upper Isles, and were now following him out to the open sea. In the distance, down below, Thor spotted Romulus's fleet blanketing the sea, and he knew that even if somehow he survived against the dragons—he would still have a million-man army to face on his own. He knew he likely would not survive this encounter. But at least it would buy the others some time.

At least Gwendolyn could make it.

\*

Gwen stood in the razed and smoldering courtyard of what remained of Tirus's court, still clutching the baby, looking up at the sky in wonder and relief and sadness all at once. Her heart soared to see Thor again, the love of her life, alive, returned, and on Mycoples, no less. With him here, she felt a part of her had been restored, felt as if anything was possible. She felt something she had not felt in a long time: the will to live again.

Her men slowly lowered their shields as they watched the dragons turn and fly off, finally leaving the Isles and heading out to open sea. Gwen looked around and saw the devastation they had left, the huge piles of rubble, the flames everywhere, and the dead dragons lying on their backs. It looked like an island ravaged by war.

Gwen also saw what must have been the baby's parents, two corpses lying nearby, right beside where Gwen had found her. Gwen looked into the baby's eyes and realized she was all she had left in the world. She clutched her tight.

"This is our chance, my lady!" Kendrick said. "We must evacuate now!"

"The dragons are distracted," Godfrey added. "For now, at least. Who knows when they shall return. We must all leave this place at once."

"But the Ring is no more," Aberthol said. "Where will we go?"

"Anywhere but here," Kendrick replied.

Gwen heard their words, yet they felt distant in her mind; she instead turned and searched the skies, watching Thor fly off in the distance, filled with longing.

"And what of Thorgrin?" she asked. "Shall we leave him, alone up there?"

Kendrick and the others grimaced, their faces falling in disappointment. Clearly, the thought disturbed them, too.

"We would fight with Thorgrin to the death if we could, my lady," Reece said. "But we cannot. He is in the sky, over the sea, far from here. None of us have a dragon. Nor do we have his power. We cannot help him. Now we must help those we can help. That is what Thor sacrificed for. That is what Thor has given his life for. We must take the opportunity he has given us."

"What remains of our fleet still lies on the far side of the island," Srog added. "It was wise of you to hide those ships. Now we must use them. Whoever is left of our people, we must leave this place at once—before their return."

Gwendolyn's mind raced with mixed emotions. She wanted so badly to go and save Thor; yet at the same time, she knew that waiting here, with all these people, would do him no good. The others were right: Thor had just given his life for their safety. It would make his actions worth nothing if she did not try to save these people while she could.

Another thought loomed in Gwen's mind: Guwayne. If they left now, rushed out to the open sea, maybe, just maybe, they could find him. And the thought of seeing her son again filled with her a new will to live.

Finally, Gwen nodded, holding the baby, preparing to move.

"Okay," she said. "Let us go and find my son."

*

The roar of the dragons grew louder behind Thor, the group getting closer, chasing them, as he and Mycoples flew farther out to sea. Thor felt a wave of flame rolling toward his back, about to engulf them, and he knew that if he did not do something soon, he would soon be dead.

Thor closed his eyes, no longer afraid to call on the power within him, no longer feeling the need to rely upon physical weapons. As he closed his eyes, he recalled his time in the Land of the Druids, recalled how powerful he had been, how much he had been able to influence everything around him with his mind. He recalled the power within him, how the physical universe was just an extension of his mind.

Thor willed his mind power to the surface, and he imagined a great wall of ice behind him, shielding him from fire, protecting him. He imagined himself completely covered in a protective bubble, he and Mycoples, safe from the dragons' wall of fire.

Thor opened his eyes and was amazed to feel himself encased in cold, and to see a tremendous wall of ice all around him, just as he'd envisioned, three feet thick and sparkling blue. He turned and watched the dragons' wall of flame approach—and get stopped by the wall of ice, the flames hissing, huge clouds of steam rising up. The dragons were irate.

Thor circled around as the wall of ice melted, and he decided to meet the nest of dragons head on. Mycoples fearlessly flew into the dragons—and clearly, they were not expecting this attack.

Mycoples lunged forward, extended her talons, grabbed one dragon by its jaw, and swung around and threw it; the dragon went hurtling, end over end, spinning out of control, and down into the ocean below.

Before she could regroup, Mycoples was attacked by another dragon, which clamped its jaws on her side. Mycoples shrieked, and Thor reacted immediately. He jumped off Mycoples's back onto the dragon's nose, and ran along its head and re-mounted himself on the dragon's back. The dragon kept its hold on Mycoples, bucking wildly to knock Thor off, and Thor held on for dear life as he rode the hostile dragon.

Mycoples lurched forward and with her jaws clamped down on the tail of another dragon, tearing it off. The dragon screamed and plummeted to the ocean—but no sooner had she done so than Mycoples was pounced on by several more dragons, who sank their teeth into her legs.

Thor, meanwhile, still held on for dear life, determined to take control of this dragon. He forced himself to remain calm and to remember that it was all a matter of his mind. He could feel the tremendous power of this ancient, primordial beast raging through his veins. And as he closed his eyes, he stopped resisting, and began to feel in tune with it. He felt its heart, its pulse, its mind. He felt himself become one with it.

Thor opened his eyes, and the dragon opened its eyes too, now glowing a different color. Thor saw the world through the dragon's eyes. This dragon, this hostile beast, became an extension of Thor. What it saw, Thor saw. Thor commanded it—and it listened.

The dragon, at Thor's command, released its grip on Mycoples; it then roared and lurched forward, sinking its teeth into the three dragons attacking Mycoples, and tearing them to pieces.

The other dragons were caught off guard, clearly not expecting one of their own to attack them; before they could regroup, Thor had already attacked a half dozen of them, using this dragon to clamp down on the back of their necks, catching them unaware, maiming one dragon after the next. Thor dove into three more and had the dragon bite down on their wings, tearing them from their backs, the dragons tumbling into the sea.

Suddenly Thor was attacked from the side, and did not see it coming; the dragon opened its jaws and sank its teeth into Thor.

Thor shrieked as a long, jagged tooth punctured his rib cage and knocked him off his dragon, sending him tumbling through the air. He felt himself plunging down toward the ocean, wounded, and he realized he was about to die.

Out of the corner of his eye, Thor spotted Mycoples diving down beneath him—and the next thing Thor knew, he landed on Mycoples's back, saved by his old friend. The two of them were back together again, both wounded.

Thor, breathing hard, clutching his rib, surveyed the damage they had done: a dozen dragons now lay dead or maimed, bobbing in the ocean. They had done well, just the two of them, far better than he would have imagined.

Yet Thor heard a tremendous shriek, and he looked up to see several dozen dragons left. Gasping for breath, Thor realized it been a valiant fight, but their chance of winning looked grim. Still, he did not hesitate; he flew fearlessly upward, racing to meet the dragons that challenged them.

Mycoples shrieked and breathed back fire as they sent fire at Thor. Thor again used his powers to put up a wall of ice before him, stopping the dragons' flames from reaching him. He held onto

Mycoples as she impacted the group, as she thrashed and clawed and bit, fighting for her life. She took wounds, but she did not let it slow her down as she wounded dragons on all sides of her. Thor, joining in, raised his bracelet and took aim at dragon after dragon, and as a beam of white light shot forth, it knocked one dragon after the next off of Mycoples as she fought.

Thor and Mycoples fought and fought, each covered in wounds, bleeding, exhausted.

And yet, still, dozens more dragons remained.

As Thor held up his bracelet, he felt the power ebbing—indeed, he felt the power ebbing from himself. He was powerful, he knew, but not powerful enough yet; he knew he could not sustain the fight until the very end.

Thor looked up to see huge wings in his face, followed by long sharp talons, and he watched helplessly as they punctured Mycoples's throat. Thor held on for dear life as the dragon grabbed hold of Mycoples, clamped its jaws down on her tail, and swung her around and threw her.

Thor hung on as he and Mycoples went spinning through the air; Mycoples tumbled end over end, and they plummeted down for the ocean, out of control.

They landed in the water, Thor still holding on, and the two of them plunged beneath the surface. Thor flailed underwater, until finally their momentum stopped. Mycoples turned and swam up, heading for sunlight.

As they surfaced, Thor breathed deep, gasping for air, treading the frigid waters as he still clung to Mycoples. The two bobbed in the water, and as they did, Thor looked to the side and saw a sight he would never forget: floating in the water, not far from him, eyes open, dead, was a dragon he had come to love: Ralibar.

Mycoples spotted him at the same time, and as she did, something overcame her, something Thor had never seen: she shrieked a great wail of grief and raised her wings high, extending them all the way. Her entire body shuddered as she let out a horrific howl, shaking the universe. Thor saw her eyes change, glowing all different colors, until finally they were shining yellow and white.

Mycoples turned, a different dragon, and looked up at the host of dragons coming down for them. Something within her, Thor realized, had snapped. Her mourning had morphed into rage, and had given her a power unlike any Thor had ever seen. She was a dragon possessed.

Mycoples raced up to the sky, wounds bleeding and not caring. Thor felt a new burst of energy as well, and a desire for vengeance. Ralibar had been a close friend, had sacrificed his life for all of them, and Thor felt determined to set wrongs right.

As they raced toward them, Thor leapt off of Mycoples and landed on the nose of the closest dragon, hugging it as he leaned around and grabbed at its jaws, clamping them shut. Thor summoned whatever power he had left within him, and he spun the dragon around in the air, then threw it with all his might. The dragon went flying, taking out two more dragons in the air, and all three went soaring down to the ocean below.

Mycoples whirled around and caught Thor as he fell, and he landed on her back as she raced for the dragons that remained. She met their roars with hers, biting stronger, flying faster, cutting deeper than they. The more they wounded her, the less she seemed to notice. She was a whirlwind of destruction, as was Thor, and by the time she and Thor were done, Thor realized there were no more dragons left in the sky to greet them: all of them had dropped down from the sky to the ocean, maimed or killed.

Thor found himself flying alone with Mycoples high in the air, circling the fallen dragons below, taking stock. The two of them breathed hard, dripping blood. Thor knew that Mycoples was breathing her dying breaths—he could see it as blood dripped from her mouth, each breath a gasp, a death pain.

"No, my friend," Thor said, holding back tears. "You cannot die."

*My time has come*, Thor heard her say. *At least I have died with dignity.*

"No," Thor insisted. "You must not die!"

Mycoples breathed blood, and the flapping of her wings weakened as she began to dip down toward the ocean.

*There is one last fight left in me*, Mycoples said. *And I want my final moment to be one of valor.*

Mycoples looked up, and Thor followed her gaze to see Romulus's fleet of ships stretching across the horizon.

Thor nodded gravely. He knew what Mycoples wanted. She wanted to greet her death in one last great battle.

Thor, badly wounded, breathing hard, feeling as if he would not make it either, wanted to go down that way, too. He wondered now if his mother's prophecies were true. She told him that he could alter his own destiny. Had he altered it? he wondered. Would he die now?

"Then let us go, my friend," Thorgrin said.

Mycoples let out a great shriek, and together, the two of them dove down, taking aim for Romulus's fleet.

Thor felt the wind and the clouds racing through his hair and face as he let out a great battle cry. Mycoples shrieked to match his rage, and they dove down low, and Mycoples opened her great jaws and breathed down fire on one ship after another.

Soon, a wall of flame spread across the seas, set one ship after another aflame. Tens of thousands of ships lay before them, but Mycoples would not stop, opening her jaws, unrolling cloud after cloud of flame. The flames stretched as if they were one continuous wall, as the screams of men rose up below.

Mycoples's flames began to weaken, and soon she breathed, and little fire emerged. Thor knew that she was dying beneath him. She flew lower and lower, too weak to breathe fire. But she was not too weak to use her body as a weapon, and in place of breathing fire, she dropped down toward the ships, aiming her hardened scales into them, like a meteor racing down from the sky.

Thor braced himself and held on with all his might as she dove right into the ships, the sound of cracking wood filling the air. She flew into one ship after another, back and forth, destroying the fleet. Thor held on as pieces of wood smashed into him from every direction.

Finally, Mycoples could go no further. She stopped in the center of the fleet, bobbing in the water, having destroyed many of the ships, yet still surrounded by thousands more. Thor bobbed on her back as she lay floating, breathing weakly.

The remaining ships turned on them. Soon the skies grew black, and Thor heard a whizzing sound. He looked up and saw a rainbow of arrows arching his way. Suddenly, he was overcome with horrific pain, pierced with the arrows, with nowhere to hide. Mycoples, too, was pierced by them, and they began to sink beneath the waves, two great heroes having fought the battle of their lives. They had destroyed the dragons and much of the Empire fleet. They had done more than an entire army could have done.

But now there was nothing left, they could die. As Thor was pierced by arrow after arrow, sinking lower and lower, he knew there was nothing left to do but prepare to die.

# CHAPTER SEVEN

Alistair looked down to find herself standing on a skywalk, and as she looked past it, down far below, she saw the ocean crashing into rocks, the sound filling her ears. A strong gale of wind knocked her off balance, and Alistair looked up and, as she had in so many dreams in her life, she saw a castle perched on a cliff, heralded by a shining gold door. Standing before it was a single figure, a silhouette, hands held out to her as if to embrace her—yet Alistair could not see her face.

"My daughter," the woman said.

She tried to take a step toward her, but her legs were stuck, and she looked down to see she was shackled to the ground. Try as she did, Alistair was unable to move.

She reached her hands out to her mother and cried desperately: "Mother, save me!"

Suddenly Alistair felt her world slipping past her, felt herself plummeting, and she looked down to see the skywalk collapsing beneath her. She fell, shackles dangling behind her, and went hurtling down toward the ocean, taking an entire section of the skywalk with her.

Alistair went numb as her body sank into the ice-cold ocean, still shackled. She felt herself sinking, and she looked up to see the daylight above become more and more faint.

Alistair opened her eyes to find herself sitting in a small, stone cell, in a place she did not recognize. Before her sat a single figure, and she dimly recognized him: Erec's father. He grimaced down at her.

"You have murdered my son," he said. "Why?"

"I did not!" she protested weakly.

He frowned.

"You shall be sentenced to death," he added.

"I did not murder Erec!" Alistair protested. She stood and tried to rush to him, but once again she found herself shackled to the wall.

There appeared behind Erec's father a dozen guards, dressed in all black armor, wearing formidable faceplates, the sound of their jingling spurs filling the room. They approached and reached out and grabbed Alistair, yanking her, pulling her from the wall. Yet her ankles were still shackled, and they stretched her body more and more.

"No!" Alistair shrieked, being torn apart.

Alistair woke, covered in a cold sweat, and looked all around, trying to figure out where she was. She was disoriented; she did not recognize the small, dim cell she sat in, the ancient stone walls, the metal bars on the windows. She spun around, trying to walk, and she heard a rattling and looked down to see her ankles were shackled to the wall. She tried to shake them loose but she could not, the cold iron cutting into her ankles.

Alistair took stock and realized that she was in a small holding cell partly beneath ground, the only light source coming from the small window cut into the stone, blocked by iron bars. There came a distant cheer, and Alistair, curious, made her way to the window, as much as the shackles allowed, and leaned forward and looked through, trying to get a glimpse of daylight, and to see where she was.

Alistair saw a huge crowd gathered—and at its head stood Bowyer, smug, triumphant.

"That sorcerer Queen tried to murder her husband-to-be!" Bowyer boomed to the crowd. "She approached me with a plot to kill Erec and to marry me instead. But her plans were foiled!"

An indignant cheer arose from the crowd, and Bowyer waited for them to calm. He raised his palms and spoke again.

"You can all rest easy now knowing that the Southern Isles shall not be under Alistair's rule, or under any other rule but my own. Now that Erec lies dying, it is I, Bowyer, who will protect you, I, the next-best champion of the games."

There came a huge shout of approval, and the crowd started to chant:

"King Bowyer, King Bowyer!"

Alistair watched the scene in horror. Everything was happening so quickly around her, she could hardly process it all. This monster, Bowyer, just the sight of him filled her with rage. This very same man who had tried to murder her beloved was right there, before her eyes, claiming to be innocent, and trying to blame her. Worst of all, he would be named King. Would there be no justice?

Yet what happened to her didn't bother her nearly as much as the thought of Erec wallowing in his sickbed, still needing her healing. She knew that if she did not complete the healing on him soon, he would die here. She didn't care if she wallowed away in this dungeon forever for a crime she did not commit—she just wanted to make sure that Erec was healed.

The door to her cell suddenly slammed open, and Alistair wheeled to see a large group of people march in. At their center was Dauphine, flanked by Erec's brother, Strom, and his mother. Behind them were several royal guards.

Alistair stood up to greet them, but her shackles dug into her ankles, rattling, sending a piercing pain through her shins.

"Is Erec okay?" Alistair asked, desperate. "Please tell me. Does he live?"

"How dare you ask if he is alive," Dauphine snapped.

Alistair turned to Erec's mother, hoping for her mercy.

"Please, just let me know that he lives," she pleaded, her heart breaking inside.

His mother nodded back gravely, looking at her with disappointment.

"He does," she said weakly. "Though he lies gravely ill."

"Bring me to him!" Alistair insisted. "Please. I must heal him!"

"*Bring you to him?*" Dauphine echoed. "The temerity. You are not going anywhere near my brother—in fact, you are not going anywhere at all. We just came to take one last look at you before your execution."

Alistair's heart fell.

"Execution?" she asked. "Is there no judge or jury on this island? Is there no system of justice?"

"*Justice?*" Dauphine said, stepping forward, red-faced. "*You* dare ask for justice? We found the bloody sword in your hand, our dying brother in your arms, and you dare to speak of justice? Justice has been served."

"But I tell you, I did not kill him!" Alistair pleaded.

"That's right," Dauphine said, her voice dripping with sarcasm, "a magical mystery man entered the room and killed him, then disappeared and placed a weapon in your hands."

"It was not a mystery man," Alistair insisted. "It was Bowyer. I saw with my own eyes. He killed Erec."

Dauphine grimaced.

"Bowyer showed us the scroll that you penned to him. You pleaded for his hand in marriage and planned to kill Erec and marry him instead. You are a sick woman. Was not having my brother and having the Queenship enough for you?"

Dauphine handed Alistair the scroll, and Alistair's heart sank as she read:

*Once Erec is dead, we shall spend our lives together.*

"But that is not my hand!" Alistair protested. "The scroll is forged!"

"Yes, I'm sure it is," Dauphine said. "I'm sure you have a convenient explanation for everything."

"I penned no such scroll!" Alistair insisted. "Don't you hear yourselves? This makes no sense. Why would I murder Erec? I love him with all my soul. We were nearly wed."

"And thank the heavens you were not," Dauphine said.

"You must believe me!" Alistair insisted, turning to Erec's mother. "Bowyer tried to kill Erec. He wants the kingship. I want nothing of being Queen. I never have."

"Don't you worry," Dauphine said. "You shall never be. In fact, you shall not even live. We here on the Southern Isles serve justice quickly. Tomorrow, you shall be executed."

Alistair shook her head, realizing they could not be reasoned with. She sighed, her heart heavy.

"Is that why you've come?" she asked weakly. "To tell me that?"

Dauphine sneered back in the silence, and Alistair could feel the hatred in her gaze.

"No," Dauphine finally replied, after a long, heavy silence. "It was to pronounce your sentence to you, and to take one long last look at your face before you are sent to hell. You will be made to suffer, the same way our brother was made to suffer."

Suddenly, Dauphine reddened, lunged forward, reached out her fingernails, and grabbed Alistair's hair. It happened so quickly, Alistair had no time to react. Dauphine let out a guttural scream as she scratched Alistair's face. Alistair raised her hands to block herself, as others stepped forward to pull Dauphine off.

"Let go of me!" Dauphine yelled. "I want to kill her now!"

"Justice will be served tomorrow," Strom said.

"Lead her out of here," Erec's mother commanded.

Guards stepped forward and yanked Dauphine from the room as she kicked and screamed in protest. Strom joined them, and soon the room was completely empty except for Alistair and Erec's mother. She stopped at the door, slowly turned, and faced Alistair. Alistair searched her face for any trace left of kindness and compassion.

"Please, you must believe me," Alistair said earnestly. "I don't care what the others think of me. But I do care about you. You were kind to me from the moment you met me. You know how much I love your son. You know I could never have done this."

Erec's mother examined her, and as her eyes watered, she seemed to vacillate.

"That is why you stayed behind, isn't it?" Alistair pressed. "That is why you've lingered. Because you want to believe me. Because you know I am right."

After a long silence, his mother finally nodded. As if coming to a decision, she took several steps toward her. Alistair could see that Erec's mother really did believe her, and she was elated.

His mother rushed forward and embraced her, and Alistair hugged her back and cried over her shoulder. Erec's mother cried, too, and finally, she stepped back.

"You must listen to me," Alistair said urgently. "I care not for what happens to me, or what others think of me. But Erec—I must get to him. *Now*. He is dying. I've only partially healed him, and I need to finish. If I do not, he will die."

His mother looked her up and down, as if finally realizing she was speaking the truth.

"After all that's happened," she said, "all you care about is my son. I can see now that you really do care for him—and that you could never have done this."

"Of course not," Alistair said. "I've been set up by that barbarian, Bowyer."

"I will get you to Erec," she said. "It may cost us our lives, but if so, we will die trying. Follow me."

49

His mother unlocked her shackles, and Alistair quickly followed her out the cell, into the dungeons, and on their way to risk it all for Erec.

# CHAPTER EIGHT

Gwendolyn stood on the bow of the ship, the ocean caressing her face, surrounded by all of her people, holding the rescued baby. All were in a state of shock as they sailed on the seas, already far from the Upper Isles. They were joined by just two ships, all that was left of the great fleet that had set sail from the Ring. Gwen's people, her nation, all the proud citizens of the Ring, had been reduced to but several hundred survivors, a nation in exile, floating, homeless, looking for some place to start again. And they were all looking to her for leadership.

Gwen stared out at the sea, examining it as she had been for hours, immune to the cold spray of the ocean mist as she peered into the fog, as she tried to keep her heart from breaking. The baby in her arms had finally fallen asleep, and all Gwen could think of was Guwayne. She hated herself; she had been so stupid to let him sail away. At the time it had seemed like the best idea, had seemed like the only way to save him from the certain imminent death. Who could have foreseen the change of events, that the dragons would have been averted? If Thor had not appeared when he had, surely they would all be dead right now—and Gwen could never have expected that.

Gwen had managed, at least, to save some of her people, some of her fleet, to save this baby, and they had managed, at least, to escape from the isle of death. Yet Gwen still shuddered each time a roar of the dragons pierced the air, growing ever distant the farther they sailed. She closed her eyes and winced; she knew there was an epic battle being waged, and that Thor was in the middle of it. More than anything, she wanted to be there, by his side. Yet at the same time, she knew that would be futile. She would be useless as Thor fought those dragons, and she would just expose her people to getting killed.

Gwen kept seeing Thor's face, and it tore her apart to see him again, only to then see him fly off just as quickly, without even a chance to speak to him, without even a moment to tell him how much she missed him, how much she loved him.

"My lady, we follow no course."

Gwendolyn turned and saw, standing beside her, Kendrick—and beside him, Reece, Godfrey, and Steffen, all looking at her. Kendrick, she realized, had been trying to talk to her for a while now, but she had barely heard his words. She looked down and saw her knuckles, white, gripping the wood, then peered out to the ocean, checking every wave, thinking time and again she spotted Guwayne, only to see that it was but another illusion in this cruel, cruel sea.

"My lady," Kendrick continued, patiently, "your people look to you for direction. We are lost. We need a destination."

Gwen looked to him sadly.

"My baby is our destination," she replied, voice heavy with grief as she turned and looked out over the rail.

"My lady, I am the first to want to find your son," Reece added, "and yet, we do not know where we sail. Any of us would risk our lives for Guwayne—yet you must acknowledge that we do not know where he is. We have been sailing north for half a day—but what if the tides carried him south? Or east? West? What if our ships right now take us farther from him?"

"You don't know that," Gwen replied, defensive.

"Exactly," Godfrey said. "We *don't* know—that is the entire point. We don't know anything. If we sail deeper into this vast ocean, we may not ever find Guwayne. And we may lead all of our people farther from a new home."

Gwendolyn turned and stared at him, her eyes cold and hard.

"Don't you ever say that," she said. "I *will* find Guwayne. If it's the last thing I do, with my last dying breath, I will find him."

Godfrey looked down, and as Gwen scanned all of their faces, she could see the grief and patience and understanding in each one. And as her flash of indignation passed, she began to realize: they loved her. They loved Guwayne. And they were right.

Gwen sighed as she wiped a tear and turned and peered into the water, wondering: had Guwayne been swallowed by a wave? A shark? Had he died from the cold? She shook her head, dreading to think of the worst scenarios.

She also wondered if they were all right: was she, indeed, leading her people to nowhere? As desperate as she was to find Guwayne, her judgment was clouded. For all she knew, she could be leading them further from him. She knew this was not the time to crumple up, as much as she may want to; now was the time to think of others, to force herself to be strong.

*Guwayne will come back to me*, she told herself. *If I don't find him now, I will find him some other way.*

Gwen forced herself to believe her thoughts as she prepared for a fateful decision; she could not go on living otherwise.

"All right," she said, turning to them, sighing heavily. "We will change course." Her tone had changed; it was now the voice of a commander, of a hardened Queen who had lost too much.

Her men all seemed relieved at her decision.

"And to where shall we set course, my lady?" Srog asked.

"Surely, we cannot return to the Upper Isles," Aberthol added. "The isles are destroyed, and the dragons may return."

"Nor can we return to the Ring," Kendrick added. "It, too, is destroyed, and Romulus's million men occupy it."

Gwendolyn thought long and hard, realizing they were all right, and feeling more homeless than she'd ever had.

"We will have to set sail to a new land, and find a new home for our people," she finally replied. "We cannot return to where we were. But before we do, first, we must return for Thorgrin."

They all looked at her in surprise.

"Thorgrin?" Srog asked. "But my lady, he's in battle with the dragons, with Romulus's army. To find him would mean to return into the heart of battle."

"Precisely," Gwendolyn replied, her voice filled with a new determination. "If I cannot find my child, at least I can find Thorgrin. I will not move on without him."

The thought of returning for Thorgrin, however irrational it might be, was the only thing allowing Gwen to, in her mind, give up the search for Guwayne and change course. Otherwise, her heart would just feel too heavy.

There was a long and heavy silence amongst her men, as each looked to the other guiltily, as if all were reluctant to say something to her.

"My lady," Srog finally said, clearing his throat, stepping forward. "We all love and admire Thor, as much as we love our own selves. He is the greatest warrior we've ever known. Even so, I fear to say, there is no way he can survive against all those dragons, against the

Empire's million men. Thorgrin set himself up as a sacrifice for us, to buy us time, to allow us to escape. We must accept his gift. We must save ourselves while we can—not kill ourselves. Any of us would give our lives for Thorgrin—and yet, I fear to say, he may not be alive when we return for him."

Gwen stared back at Srog, long and hard, something hardening within her, the only sound the breeze rippling on the ocean waters.

Finally, she came to a decision, a fresh strength in her eyes.

"We are not going anywhere until I find my Thorgrin," she said. "I have no home without him. If it brings us into the heart of battle, into the very depths of hell, then that is where we shall go. He gave us his life—and we owe him ours."

Gwen did not wait for their response. She turned her back, holding the baby to her chest, and peered into the water, signaling their conversation was done. She heard footsteps behind her as the men slowly dispersed; she heard commands ordered, heard them to begin to turn about the ship, as she'd requested.

Before they turned, Gwen peered one last time into layers of fog so thick, she could not even see the horizon. She wondered what lay beyond, if anything. Was Guwayne out there, somewhere beyond? Or was there nothing but a vast and empty sea? As Gwen watched, she saw a small rainbow appear in the midst of the fog, and she felt her heart breaking. She felt that Guwayne was with her. That he was giving her a sign. And she knew she would never, ever stop searching until she found him.

Behind her, Gwen heard the creaking of ropes, the hoisting of sails, and she slowly felt the ship turn, heading in the opposite direction. She felt her heart remaining behind as she unwillingly was brought back in the other direction. She looked back, the entire time, over her shoulder, staring at the rainbow, wondering: was Guwayne somewhere beyond?

*

Guwayne rocked alone in the small boat in the vast sea, carried on the waves, up and down, as he had been for hour after hour, the ocean current pulling him in no particular direction. Above him the tattered canvas sail whipped aimlessly in the wind. Guwayne, on his back, looked straight up at it, and he watched it, mesmerized.

Guwayne had stopped crying long ago, ever since he had lost sight of his mother, and he now lay there, wrapped in his blanket, all alone in the empty sea, without his parents, with nothing left but the rocking of the waves and this tattered sail.

The rocking of his boat had relaxed him—and as it suddenly stopped, he felt a rush of panic. The bow stopped moving as it lodged itself firmly on a beach, in the sand, the waves bringing it ashore. It landed on a foreign, exotic isle way north of the Upper Isles, near the far northern edge of the Empire. Upset from the rocking motion being over, Guwayne, his boat stuck in the sand, began to cry.

Guwayne cried and cried, until the cry evolved into a piercing wail. No one came to answer him.

Guwayne looked up and saw great birds—vultures—circling again and again, looking down at him, getting closer and closer. Sensing danger, his wails increased.

One of the birds dived down for him, and Guwayne braced himself; but suddenly it flapped its wings, startled by something, and flew away.

A moment later, Guwayne saw a face looking down at him—then another, then another. Soon, dozens of faces, exotic faces, from a primitive tribe, with huge ivory hoops through their noses, stared down at him. Guwayne's cries increased as they jabbed spears at his boat. Guwayne screamed louder and louder. He wanted his mother.

"A sign from the seas," one of the men said. "Just as our prophecies have foretold."

"It is a gift from the God of Amma," another said.

"The gods must want an offering," said another.

"It is a test! We must give back what is given to us," said another.

"We must give back what is given to us!" repeated the rest, clacking their spears against the boat.

Guwayne wailed louder and louder, but it didn't do any good. One of them reached down, a tall skinny man wearing no shirt, with green skin and glowing yellow eyes, and scooped Guwayne up.

Guwayne shrieked at the feel of his skin, like sandpaper, as the man held him tight and breathed down his bad breath on him.

"A sacrifice for Amma!" he cried.

The men cheered, and as one they all turned and began to carry Guwayne away from the beach, toward the mountains, their sights set on the far side of the island, on the volcano, still smoking. None of them stopped to turn around, to look back at the ocean from which they'd left.

But if they had, even for an instant, they would have seen an unusually thick fog, a rainbow in its center, hardly fifty yards away. Behind them, unnoticed by anyone, the fog slowly lifted until finally the skies were clear, revealing three ships, turning around, all with their backs to the island, and all sailing the other way.

# CHAPTER NINE

Thor lay atop Mycoples, both bobbing in the waves, slowly sinking into the ocean, completely surrounded by the Empire's fleet. Thor lay there, his body pierced by dozens of arrows, dripping blood, in excruciating pain. He felt the life force seeping out of him, and as he held onto Mycoples, he felt her life force leaving her, too. There was blood in the water everywhere, and small, glowing fish came to the surface and lapped it up.

Slowly, they sank, the water submerging Thor up to his ankles, then his knees, then his stomach, as Mycoples sank and went under. Neither had the strength to resist.

Finally, Thor let himself go and he went under, his head dunking beneath the surface, too weak to stop it. As he did, he heard the distant sound of arrows piercing the water, striking him even beneath the surface. Thor felt as if he were being struck by thousands of them, as if everyone he'd ever fought in battle was taking their vengeance. He wondered, as he sank further, why he had to suffer this much before he died.

As Thor sank deeper and deeper toward the bottom of the ocean, he felt his life could not end this way. It was too soon. He had too much left to live. He wanted more time with Gwendolyn; he wanted to marry her. He wanted time with Guwayne; he wanted to watch him grow up. Wanted to teach him what it meant to be a great warrior.

Thor had barely begun to live, had just stepped into his true stride as a warrior and as a Druid, and now his life was ending. He had finally met his mother, who had granted him powers greater than he'd ever known, and who had foreseen more quests for him—even greater quests. She had also seen him become a King. Yet she had also seen how his destiny could be changed at any moment. Had she been seeing truly? Or was his life really meant to end now?

Thor willed that he not die, with every ounce of his being. As he did, he recalled his mother's words: *You are destined to die twelve times. Each moment, fate will intervene, or it will not. It will depend on you, and whether you've passed the test. These moments of death might also become moments of life.*

*You will be supremely tested and tormented. More than any warrior has ever been tested before. If you have the internal strength to withstand it. Ask yourself, how much suffering can you tolerate? The more you can handle, the greater you will become.*

As Thor felt himself sinking, he wondered: was this one of those tests? Was this one of his twelve deaths? He felt that it was, that it was a supreme test of physical strength and courage and stamina. As he sank, his body pierced by arrows, he did not know if he was strong enough to pass it.

Thor, his lungs bursting, was determined to summon a reserve strength. He was determined to become bigger than he was, to tap into some internal power.

*You are bigger than your body. Your spirit is greater than your strength. Strength is finite; spirit knows no bounds.*

Thor suddenly opened his eyes underwater, feeling a burning heat within him, feeling himself reborn. He kicked, overcoming the pain of the arrows piercing his body, and forced himself to swim to the surface. Covered with arrows, he swam and swam, heading for daylight, his lungs bursting, and finally he surfaced, like a giant porcupine, from the waters, gasping for air.

Thor used his power and momentum, and with a great shriek he lifted up into the air and landed on the deck of the nearest boat, on his feet.

Thor summoned some ancient part of himself, and he turned off the pain. He reached over, grabbed the arrows piercing his arms, shoulders, chest, thighs, and two, three, four at a time, he yanked them out. He shrieked a great battle cry, and he felt bigger than the pain as he removed every arrow.

Standing before Thor were two shocked Empire soldiers, who stared back at him, eyes wide in fear. Thor reached out, grabbed them both, and smashed them together, knocking them out.

Thor charged the group of soldiers on the ship; he kicked the one closest to him, sending him stumbling backwards into the others—but not before he snatched the sword from the soldier's scabbard. Thor raised the sword high and charged forward into the stunned crowd, slashing and killing everyone in his path. They tried to fight back, but Thor was like a whirlwind, racing through the ship, killing two soldiers before one had time to try to block a blow.

Thor raced through the ship and he fought and fought until there was not a soul left on board. As Thor reached the bow, he looked out and found himself facing Romulus, on the bow of another ship, who was staring back at him in shock. Thor did not hesitate; he let out a shriek as he pulled back his sword and threw it.

The sword spun end over end, shimmering in the light, aiming right for Romulus.

Romulus, still in shock, realized what was happening too late, and turned his back and tried to run.

Romulus dodged as he ran, trying to escape the deadly blow—and he spared himself a certain death. But he was not quick enough to escape injury: the sword grazed his head and sliced off one of Romulus's ears.

Romulus shrieked as he sank to his knees and reached up to his missing ear, blood gushing down on his fingers.

Thor grimaced back. At least he had some satisfaction—yet still Romulus was not dead.

Suddenly, all of the Empire soldiers on the other ships began to regroup, and they fired arrows and hurled spears at Thorgrin, who stood there, exposed.

Thor saw them all coming, a sea of black ready to kill him, and this time, he closed his eyes and raised his palms and summoned an inner power. He cast an orb of light around him, a yellow shield, and as the arrows and spears neared, they bounced harmlessly off it.

Thor stood there, invincible, in the midst of all these men, and he leaned back and raised his palms to the sky—determined to kill them all.

Thor felt the energy of the sky entering his palms; he also felt the energy of the ocean below, mirroring the heavens. Thor felt one with the power running through the universe; it was a great current, greater than he could ever imagine. He felt the very fabric of the air, of the waters, and he felt that he could harness it.

*Heavens rage; oceans churn,* Thor commanded silently. *I will you. For the sake of justice. Purge this evil I see before me, once and for all.*

As Thor stood there, slowly, he could feel something happening: he felt a great wind pick up, tickling his palms, and as he opened his eyes, he watched as the sunny day turned black. Thick, dark clouds rolled in, thunder clapped, and lightning flashed. The waters churned, and his ship began to rock and sway as the ocean became stormy.

Another clap of thunder, and Thor felt the waves get stronger, his ship rising and falling, as the wind became louder and rain fell.

*Universe, I summon you. You are one with me. And I with you. Your fight is my fight, and my battle is your battle.*

Thor let out a great shriek, and the entire horizon lit with lightning, not disappearing. Thunder clapped again and again, so loud it shook the boats, and Romulus and all the Empire turned, fear in their eyes, and faced the horizon lit by lightning.

Thor watched with awe as suddenly, a massive tidal wave came their way.

Romulus and the others all cried out in terror as they raised their arms to their faces, cowering.

But there was nothing they could do. They were in the path of the wrath of the seas, and as the great wave rushed forward, in moments the ships were all caught up in it, climbing higher and higher to its crest, getting lost, like ants in the great wave.

It was the biggest wave Thor had ever seen—as tall as a mountain—and he, too, became caught up in it, rising and rising with the rest of the Empire fleet. Thor rose a hundred feet, then another hundred, and another—and he watched in shock as the wave began to crash, as he began to plummet down with all the others, his stomach dropping. The shrieks of all the Empire were drowned out by the wind and the rain, and Thor's shriek, too, was swallowed up. As he looked down, plummeting back into the ocean, he knew the impact would crush him. He had summoned a storm that even he could not control.

As Thor prepared to die, once again, he felt that, if he could take any solace in his death, it was that he had, at least, taken the Empire out with him.

*Thank you, God,* he thought, *for this victory.*

# CHAPTER TEN

Alistair followed Erec's mother through the night, as she led her in the darkness, twisting and turning down the narrow alleyways of court, her heart pounding as she tried to keep up and not be seen. Long shadows were cast across the stone walls and paths, the only illumination coming from the sporadic torchlight, and Alistair, freshly escaped, could not help but feel like a criminal.

His mother finally led her behind a wall and crouched down low, out of sight of the guards, and Alistair squatted down beside her. They crouched in silence, listening, watching the guards pass by, and Alistair prayed they would not get caught. Erec's mother had waited until nightfall to lead her here, so that they would not be detected, and they had twisted and turned down the series of labyrinthine streets and back alleys that led the way from the dungeons to the royal house of the sick, where Erec lay. Finally, they were close, close enough that Alistair, peeking around the corner, could see its entrance. It was well guarded, a dozen men standing before it.

"Look at that door," Alistair whispered to his mother. "Why would Bowyer keep it so well guarded if he was really convinced I am the one that tried to kill Erec? He has positioned these men here not to protect Erec—but to prevent him from escaping, or to kill him, should he recover."

Erec's mother's nodded in understanding.

"It will not be easy to get you past the guards," she whispered back. "Lower your hood, lower your eyes, keep your head down. Do as I tell you. If this does not work, they will kill you. Are you willing to take that chance?"

Alistair nodded back.

"For Erec, I would give up my life."

Erec's mother looked back at her, touched.

"You could escape if you choose, yet instead you risk your life to heal Erec. You really do love him, don't you?" she asked.

Alistair's eyes filled with tears.

"More than I can say."

Erec's mother took her hand, suddenly stepped out from behind the wall, and led Alistair right up to the main doors of the building, walking proudly, straight down the middle, right to the guards.

"My Queen," said one.

They all bowed and began to allow her through, when suddenly one guard stepped forward.

"Who accompanies you, my lady?" he asked.

"Dare you question your Queen?" she snapped back, her voice made of steel. "Dare speak like that again, and you shall be removed from your post."

"I am sorry, my lady," he said, "but I follow the chain of command."

"Whose command?"

"The new King, my lady—Bowyer's."

The Queen sighed.

"I shall forgive you this time," she said. "If my husband, the former king, were alive, he would not be so kind. So you know," she added, "this is my dear friend. She has fallen ill, and I am leading her to the sickhouse."

"I am sorry, my lady," the guard said, his head low, reddening, and stepped aside.

They opened the doors for her and Erec's mother rushed in, holding Alistair's hand, and Alistair, heart pounding, keeping her head down, heard the door slam closed behind them.

Erec's mother reached up and pulled back her hood. Alistair looked around and saw they were inside the house of the sick, a beautiful marble building, with low ceilings, dimly lit by torches.

"We have not much time," she said. "Follow me."

Alistair followed her down the halls, twisting and turning, until finally his mother instructed her to raise her hood, and approached Erec's door. This time, the guard stepped aside without any questions, and his mother strutted in, holding Alistair's hand.

"All of you, leave us," Erec's mother commanded the guards in the room. "I wish to be alone with my son."

Alistair kept her head down, waiting, her heart pounding, hoping no one detected her. She heard the shuffling of feet as several guards filtered out of the room, and finally, she heard the slamming of the wooden door behind her, and an iron bolt being slid into place.

Alistair pulled back her hood and scanned the room immediately, looking for Erec. It was a dim room, lit by a single torch, and Erec lay in a kingly bed on the opposite side, beneath piles of luxurious furs, his face more pale than she'd ever seen it.

"Oh, Erec," Alistair said, rushing forward, bursting into tears at the sight of him. She detected his energy before she even got close, and it was a death energy. She sensed his life force on the way out. She had been away from him for too long. Alistair knew she should not be surprised; the first healing she'd given him had only been enough to immediately revive him. He had needed a longer session of healing to prevent him from dying, and so much time had passed.

Alistair rushed to his side, knelt down, and grabbed his hand in hers, leaning it on her forehead as she wept. He was cold to the touch. He did not stir, did not even flutter his eyes. He lay perfectly still, as if already dead.

"Is it too late?" his mother asked as she knelt by the other side of the bed, panic-stricken.

Alistair shook her head.

"There might still be time," she replied.

Alistair leaned over and placed both her palms on Erec's chest, slipping them through his shirt, feeling his bare skin. She could feel his heart beating, though faintly, and she leaned over him and closed her eyes.

Alistair summoned every power she'd ever had, willing herself to bring Erec back to life. As she did, she felt a tremendous heat rushing through her arms, through her palms, then felt it leaving her body and entering Erec's. She watched her hands turn black, and realized how desperately Erec needed this.

Alistair remained there for she did not know how long.

She did not know how many hours had passed when she finally opened her eyes, feeling something subtle shift within her. She looked down and saw Erec open his eyes for the first time. He looked right at her.

"Alistair," he whispered.

He raised a weakened hand and clasped her wrist.

Alistair wept, and his mother wept, too.

"You've come back to us," his mother said.

Erec turned and looked at her.

63

"Mother," he said.

Erec's eyes closed again, and he was clearly still weak and exhausted; yet Alistair could see his skin turning back to its old color, could see the life force once again flowing within him. Slowly, his cheeks came back to color, too. She was elated, yet drained.

"He will be weak for quite a while," Alistair said. "It could be weeks before he can stand and walk. But he will live."

Alistair leaned over, exhausted, nearly collapsing on the bed, all her energy taken from her. She knew that she, too, would need a long time to recover.

Erec's mother gave Alistair a look of profound love and gratitude.

"You saved my son," she said. "I can see now how wrong I was. I can see now that you had nothing to do with his attempted murder."

"I would never lay a hand on him."

Erec's mother nodded.

"And now you must prove that to our people."

"This entire island has me convicted," Alistair said.

"I will not let them," his mother insisted. "You are like a daughter to me. After tonight, I would send myself to the dungeons before you."

"But how can I prove my innocence?" she asked.

His mother thought for a long time, and slowly her eyes lit up.

"There is one way," she finally said. "One way you can prove it to them."

Alistair looked at her, her heart pounding.

"Tell me," she said.

His mother sighed.

"We Southern Islanders have a right to challenge. If you challenge Bowyer to the Drink of Truth, he will have no choice but to agree."

"What is that?" Alistair asked.

"It is an ancient rite, practiced by my forefathers. On the highest cliff, we have a fountain with magical waters, the waters of truth. Whoever lies and drinks from it will die. You can challenge Bowyer to the drink. He cannot refuse, or else be assumed to be lying. And if he is lying, as you say, then the waters will kill him—and prove your innocence."

She looked back at Alistair meaningfully.

"Are you prepared to drink?" she asked.

Alistair nodded back, elated at the chance to prove herself, elated that Erec would live, and knowing that her life was about to change forever.

# CHAPTER ELEVEN

Romulus opened his eyes slowly, awakened finally by the sound of crashing waves, and the feel of something crawling across his face. He looked up to see a large, purple crab, with four eyes, crawling slowly on his face. He recognized it immediately: it was a crab native to the mainland of the Ring. It narrowed its four eyes and opened its jaw to bite him.

Romulus reacted instantly, reaching up, grabbing it in his palm, and crushing it slowly. Its claws pierced his flesh, but he didn't care. He listened to it scream, and he delighted in the sound of its pain, continuing to squeeze it deliberately and slowly. It bit and pinched him, but he didn't mind. He wanted to crush the life out of it, to prolong its suffering as much as he could.

Finally, its juices dripping down his palm, the creature died, and Romulus chucked it to the sand, disappointed its fight was done so quickly.

Another wave crashed, this one rolling over the back of his head, over his face, and Romulus jumped up, covered in sand, shook off the freezing water, and looked around.

Romulus saw he'd been passed out, washed up on a beach, and recognized it as the shore of the Ring. He turned and saw thousands of corpses, all washed up onto shore, as far as the eye could see. They were all his men, thousands of them, all dead, all washed up, unmoving on the beach.

He turned and saw thousands more floating in the waves, lifeless, slowly being washed up with the others. Sharks nipped at their bodies, and all up and down the shore was a blanket of purple crabs, feasting, devouring the corpse's flesh.

Romulus looked out at the sea, so calm now, at the sunrise of a perfect, clear day, and he tried to remember. There was a storm, that wave, greater than anything he imagined could exist. His entire fleet had been destroyed, like playthings of the ocean. Indeed, as he scanned the waters, he saw it littered with debris, wood from his former ships floating up and down the shoreline, what remained of his fleet butting against the corpses of his men, like a cruel joke. Romulus felt something on his ankles, and looked down to see the remnants of a mast smashing against his shin.

Romulus was grateful and amazed to be alive. He realized how lucky he was, the sole survivor of all his men. He looked up, and even though it was morning, he could see the waxing moon, and he knew his moon cycle had not ended—and that was the only reason he had survived. Yet he was also filled with dread as he examined the shape of the moon: his cycle was almost up. That sorcerer's spell would end any day, and his invincible time would come to an end.

Romulus reflected on his dragons, dead, on his fleet, destroyed, and he realized he had made a mistake to pursue Gwendolyn. He had pushed too hard, for too much; he had never expected the power of Thorgrin. He realized now, too late, that he should have been content with what he'd had. He should have stayed on the mainland of the Ring.

Romulus turned and looked out at the Ring, the Wilds framing the shore, and beyond that, the Canyon. At least he still had his soldiers here, the ones he'd left behind; at least he still had one million men occupying it, and at least he had razed it to the ground. At least Gwendolyn and her people could never return here—and at least the Ring was finally his. It was a bittersweet victory.

Romulus turned his gaze back to the sea, and he realized that now, without his dragons, without a fleet, he would have to give up chasing Gwendolyn—especially with his moon cycle coming to an end. He would have no choice now but to return to the Empire—with a partial victory, but with the shame of defeat, the shame of a vanquished fleet. Humiliated yet again. When asked where his fleet was, he would have nothing left to show his people—just the one measly ship he had left on the Ring to transport him back to the Empire. He would return as conqueror of the Ring—and yet deeply humiliated. Once again, Gwendolyn had escaped him.

Romulus leaned back, held his fists out to the heavens, and shook them, the veins bulging in his neck as he shrieked in rage:

"THORGRIN!"

His cry was met by a lone eagle, circling high, that screeched back, as if mocking him.

# CHAPTER TWELVE

Thor opened his eyes slowly to the light sound of lapping waves, bobbing up and down, not sure where he was. He squinted at the daylight, and saw that he was lying on his stomach, bent over a plank of wood, floating in the middle of the ocean on a piece of debris. He was shivering, cold in these waters, and he looked up to see dawn breaking, and realized he had been floating here all night long.

Thor felt a light nipping on his arm, and he looked down and saw a fish and brushed it away. A light wave wet his hair, and he lifted his head, spit out the seawater and looked all around him. The sea was littered with debris as far as Thor could see, thousands of broken planks from Romulus's fleet blanketing the ocean. He was floating right in the middle of it all, with no land in sight on any horizon.

Thor tried to remember. He closed his eyes and saw himself on Mycoples, diving down, fighting Romulus's men. He remembered being underwater, pierced by arrows, then rising up; he remembered summoning the storm. And the last thing he remembered was the immense tidal wave coming down on them all. He remembered being caught in the wave, and about to crash hundreds of feet into the ocean below. He remembered the screams of all Romulus's men.

And then all was blackness.

Thor opened his eyes fully and rubbed his head, his hair caked with salt; he had a tremendous headache, and as he looked around, he realized he was the only survivor, floating alone in the midst of an endless sea, surrounded by nothing but debris. He shook from the cold, and his body stung all over, littered with arrow wounds, and scratches from the dragons' talons. He was injured so badly, he barely had the strength to lift his head.

He searched every direction, hoping for a sign of land, maybe Gwendolyn and her fleet—anything.

But there was nothing. Just vast, limitless ocean in every direction.

Thor's heart sank as he lowered his head again, half submerged in the water, and lay there, bent over the plank. The small fish returned, nipping at his skin, brushing up against it, and this time Thor didn't care. He was too weak to brush it away. He lay there, floating, realizing that Mycoples, whom he had loved more than he could say, was dead. Ralibar was dead. And Thor himself felt like he was dying. He was weaker than he had ever been, alone in an empty sea. He had survived the storm, had saved Gwendolyn and her people, had taken vengeance on the Empire, had destroyed the host of dragons, and for that he felt immense satisfaction.

Yet now that the great battle was over, here he was, injured, too weak to heal himself, with no land in sight, and no hope left. He had paid the ultimate price, and now his time had come.

More than anything, Thor ached to see Gwendolyn one last time before he died; he ached to see Guwayne. He could not imagine dying without laying eyes on their faces one more time.

*Please, God*, he thought. *Give me one more chance. One more life. Allow me to live. Allow me to see Gwendolyn, to see my son again.*

Thor lowered his head in the water as he felt more fish begin to nip, now at his feet and ankles and thighs; he felt his head submerged a bit lower in the cool water, the soft lapping of the waves the only sound left in the endless morning stillness. He felt so exhausted, so stiff, he knew he could not go on any further. He had served his purpose in life. He had served it well. And now his time had come.

*Please, God, I turn to you, and to you alone. Answer me.*

Suddenly, there came a tremendous stillness in the universe, so quiet, so intense, that Thor could hear himself breathe. That stillness terrified him more than anything he'd ever encountered in his life. He felt it was the sound of God.

The stillness was shattered by an immense splashing noise. Thor opened his eyes wide and looked up to see the ocean part. He saw an enormous whale, larger than any creature he seen his life, and different than any whale he'd ever seen. It was completely white, with horns on its head and all down its back, and huge glowing red eyes.

The beast shot out of the ocean, letting out a great screech, and opened its jaws, so big they blocked out the sun. It rose higher and higher, then came down, right for Thor, its mouth wide open. The world became dark as Thor felt the whale was about to swallow him.

Thor, too weak to resist, embraced his fate, as the immense jaws of darkness clamped down on him, swallowing him. He slid into the blackness of the whale's mouth, and as he began to slide down its throat, its stomach, his final thought was: *I never thought I would die like this.*

# CHAPTER THIRTEEN

Gwen, standing at the bow of her ship, leaned over, clutched the baby, and peered into the ocean, searching for any sign of Thorgrin. On all sides of the ship her men also examined the waters.

"THORGRIN!" called out the sailors all around the ship—and this was echoed by the sailors on the other two other ships of her fleet. The three ships, spread a good hundred yards from each other, combed the waters together, all shouting Thor's name. From the top of the masts, they tolled the bells, all three of them, intermittently, looking for any sign of him.

Gwendolyn felt like weeping inside. She had been unable to find Guwayne, and now she had no sign of Thor. She hated this ocean, cursed the day that she ever set sail from the Ring. She knew her chances were grim. Thor and Mycoples had ridden fearlessly into battle, one dragon against dozens, and even if they managed to vanquish them, how could Thor defeat Romulus's entire fleet? How could he possibly survive?

At the same time, Gwendolyn knew, by sailing in this direction, she was endangering her men, bringing them closer and closer to Romulus's fleet.

Gwen heard a sudden cracking noise down below at the hull, and she looked over the edge, startled. Below she spotted debris—planks, an old mast, a remnant of a sail… She scanned the waters, looking closely, and saw a vast sea of debris.

"What can it be?" came the voice.

Gwendolyn turned to see Kendrick by her side, Reece coming up on her other side, along with Godfrey and Steffen, all of them joining her and looking down in wonder.

"Look! The Empire banner!" Steffen called out, pointing.

Gwen looked, saw the soiled and torn flag, and realize he was correct.

"This is Empire debris," Reece said, stating what was on everyone's minds.

"But how?" Godfrey asked. "The entire Empire fleet destroyed? How is it possible?"

Gwen searched the skies for any sign of Thorgrin, wondering. Had he done this?

"It was Thorgrin," Gwen said, hoping it to be true, *willing* it to be true. "He destroyed them all."

"Then where is he?" Kendrick asked. The bells continued to toll as they headed south, further out into this sea. "I see no sign of Mycoples."

"I do now know," Gwen replied. "But even if Mycoples is dead, Thor might be alive. If there is debris, Thor might be floating on it."

"My lady," came a voice.

She turned to see Aberthol standing close by.

"I love Thorgrin as much as anyone here. But you do realize we are sailing closer and closer to the Empire. Even if Romulus's fleet is destroyed, surely his million-man army remains on the mainland of the Ring. We cannot head back to the Ring. We must find a new home, set sail in a new direction. You want to find Thorgrin, and I admire that. But it's been days, and still we have no sign of him. We have limited provisions. Our people are starving. They're homeless, have lost loved ones, and are mad with grief. They are desperate for direction. We need food and shelter. We are running out of provisions."

She knew he was right. Her people needed another direction.

"Our people need you," Srog added.

Gwen stared out into the horizon, holding the baby, and still there was no sign of Thor. She closed her eyes, wiping a tear, and she willed God to answer. Why did life have to be so hard?

*Please, God, tell me where he is. I will give you anything. Just let me save him. If I cannot save my son, let me save him. Please, don't let me lose them both.*

Gwendolyn waited, very still, hoping for a response. She opened her eyes, hoping for a sign, anything, something.

But none came.

She felt hollowed out. Abandoned.

Resolved, she finally turned and nodded to her men.

"Turn the fleet around," she said. "We shall sail this time for land."

"Turn the fleet!" echoed up and down the ships.

Everyone turned and looked in their new direction, except for Gwendolyn. She kept herself facing the direction they were sailing away from, her heart breaking, hoping for any sign of Thor.

As they began to drift further and further away, the debris getting smaller, Gwen felt every good thing left in the world being stripped from her. Was that what it meant to be Queen? Did it mean you cared more for your people than for your family? For your very own self? At this moment, being Queen was what Gwendolyn no longer wanted. At this moment, she hated her people, hated everything about being Queen. She wanted only Thorgrin and her son, and nothing else.

But as they set sail in a new direction, as the bells tolled on the masts, she knew it was not meant to be, and they felt like bells tolling on her heart.

# CHAPTER FOURTEEN

Thor tried to grab onto something, anything, as he felt himself sliding down a slimy tunnel, in a gush of liquid and seawater—but there was nothing to hang onto. As the world rushed by him in this cacophonous tunnel, he realized he was being washed down into the belly of this beast. The blackness deepened, and he braced himself for death.

Thor slid deeper and deeper down the contours of the beast's endlessly long throat—it felt like hundreds of feet—until finally he found himself ejected into a huge cavernous space. He went flying through the air, shouting as he plummeted a good twenty feet, until he finally landed in a pool of water, up to his knees, on a soft surface. He realized he must have landed on the whale's soft stomach.

As Thor lay in the shallow water, wondering if he was dead, he heard his own breathing echo in the blackness; water swished gently back and forth on the whale's stomach as it moved through the sea. Thor imagined the whale swimming through the ocean, turning side to side, diving up and down. He could faintly hear all the sounds of the ocean outside, dim from here, muted.

Thor tried to stand but stumbled as the whale raced along the ocean. There came a loud gushing noise, and Thor looked up and felt a gush of water come down on his head, along with several fish flying down through the air, landing in the belly with him. Some of them were luminescent fish, and as they landed they emitted a soft glow, lighting up the whale's belly. Thor could finally see in here, no longer in utter blackness.

A part of him wished he was. Thor looked up and was repulsed by the inner lining of the whale's belly, skin hanging off of it in pieces, remnants of dead fish and insects clinging to it, and on its floor. Strange valves opened and closed, muscles and intestines contracted and expanded, emitting bad odors, and Thor took it all in in wonder.

Thor leaned his head back against the stomach wall and breathed deeply, exhausted; his wounds were still killing him, and he felt as if he'd come to the depths of his life. He sensed there was no way out of here; he had finally come to the end.

Thor closed his eyes and shook his head.

*Why, God? Why am I being tested like this?*

Thor lay there for a very long time in the darkness, and finally he heard an answer. It was a small voice, inside his head.

*Because you are a great warrior. The greatest warriors are always tested the most.*

"But have I not already proven myself?" Thor asked aloud.

*Each time you prove yourself, you will be tested again. Each time, the tests will become greater. The more you struggle, the greater person you can become. Each test is not a difficulty—it is a precious opportunity. Be thankful for it. The more you suffer, the more thankful you must be.*

Thor leaned his head back, exhausted, slipping away to the blackness, feeling his life force ebb, and he tried to be grateful. It was hard, so hard. He felt as if he'd already lived many lifetimes, and he was deeply exhausted.

There came another gushing sound, and Thor looked up and saw more water rush down into the belly of the whale, and yet more fish, along with other strange sea animals. This whale's appetite obviously was insatiable.

With each gush of water, Thor felt the water level rising, felt it rise from his ankles to his knees as he lay along the side of the wall. There came still another gush of water, and the level rose again, now up to his thighs. Thor knew that if he did not get out of here soon, he would drown in this awful place.

Drained from his wounds, Thor could barely keep his eyes open. If he were destined to die here, he realized, then so be it. For now, there was nothing more he could do than allow his heavy eyes to close, allow himself to be carried away by sweet sleep.

Thor's eyes opened and closed as he moved in and out of consciousness for he did not know how long. He saw flashes, memories, perhaps glimpses of the future. He saw Mycoples's face, then Ralibar's. He saw himself flying on Mycoples, under a perfect clear sky, Mycoples happier than he'd ever seen her. He saw them both criss-crossing each other, flying beside each other, both of them young and healthy and happy. He could feel how much they loved him.

Thor looked down into Mycoples's face.

"I'm sorry that I let you down," he said.

*You've never let me down, Thorgrin. You gave me a chance to truly live.*

Thor blinked and found himself standing in the skywalk, in the Land of the Druids. But this time, he was not facing his mother's castle, but facing the mainland, walking *away* from the castle, his back to it. His mother, he sensed, was somewhere behind him, and yet as much as he wanted to, he was unable to look back.

"Go, Thorgrin," came her voice. "It is time for you to walk. Alone. It is time for you to leave this place, to venture out into the world. Only out in the world, on an unknown path, will you become a great warrior."

Thor took one step down the skywalk, then the next. Step by step, he walked alone, away from the castle, from the cliff, feeling his mother's presence behind him but unable to turn back. He did not know where the path would take him, but he knew he was meant to be on it.

Thor blinked and found himself standing on a foreign shore with bright yellow sand, a million small stones sparkling within it. He saw a small, lone boat on the shore, and a small baby inside, crying. Thor walked over to it and leaned down, his heart pounding at the thought of seeing his son again.

He looked down and his heart lifted to see Guwayne, looking back with Thor's same gray eyes. Thor reached out to grab him.

As he did, suddenly, savage tribesmen appeared and snatched the boy away, and turned and ran. Thor watched in horror as dozens of tribesmen ran off with Guwayne, screaming and reaching out for him.

"NO!" Thor yelled.

He tried to run for him, but he looked down to find his feet stuck in the sand.

Suddenly, the sand opened up, and Thor was sucked down into the sand, which turned to waters, and sucked back into the ocean. He sank, shrieking, lower and lower, sinking into the blackness.

Thor opened his eyes to hear another gushing of water, and he looked up to see water once again pouring down from the whale's throat to its belly, filling it up. He looked down and saw the water was now up to his chest.

Thor, still breathing hard from his nightmare, tried to escape the rising tide—but the next gush brought the water up to his throat. Thor realized that his time here was scarce. In a few moments, he would drown.

Thor closed his eyes and thought of Gwendolyn, of Guwayne, of all those he'd known and loved. He thought of his son, needing him; of Gwendolyn, needing him. He felt the bracelet on his wrist, and he thought of his mother, of Alistair, of Ralibar and Mycoples. No one would know that he died down here.

*I must do it for them*, Thor thought. *I must live for them.*

Thor opened his eyes and felt himself infused with a sudden surge of strength. He sensed the very fabric of this whale, could sense that they were all a part of the same universe. And that he could change that universe.

Thor closed his eyes and raised his palms overhead, and he felt tremendous heat emanating from them. Beams of light shot forth from them, into the belly of the whale, and they became like ropes, pulling Thor up, just before the next wave of water drowned him, high above the water, higher and higher. He soon dangled above the pool of water below, and as he swung there, he focused.

*I command you, whale. Rise to the surface. Let me out. Because I deserve to live. For everyone I've ever known in my life, for everyone who ever sacrificed for me, and for everyone who I will ever sacrifice for, I deserve to live.*

There came a distant roar, echoing inside the belly, and Thor suddenly felt the whale change direction, turning upward, shooting up at full speed, heading for the surface. It rose faster and faster, the lights from Thor's palms keeping him dangling from the ceiling as he held on.

Finally, the whale broke the surface and Thor felt it rising in the air in a high arc, and then landing back on the surface, splashing, its entire belly shaking.

It sat there, still, flat on the surface of the ocean, and as Thor peered into its throat, he suddenly saw daylight. The whale opened its jaws, light flooding in through its massive teeth, and as it did, Thor released himself from the ceiling and dove into the whale's throat.

This time the flood of waters took him back down the whale's throat, toward sunlight. Thor went sliding along, back down the whale's long, slimy tongue, slipping every which way.

Thor soon found himself sliding through the whale's teeth, out of his mouth, and back out into daylight, onto the surface of the water.

Thor flailed in the open ocean, startled by how cold it was, and he reached out and grabbed onto several wooden planks of debris. As he lay there, floating, Thor turned and looked at the beast.

The whale stared back at Thor with its immense eye, unblinking, an ancient eye which seemed to hold all the knowledge and secrets of the world. It remained there, floating on the surface, examining Thor as if he were an old friend.

Finally, without warning, it lowered its head and dipped below the water, disappearing just as quickly as it had appeared. Thor was rocked by the waves left in its wake.

Thor, all alone again, floated there, exhausted, bent over the piece of debris. He looked out to the ocean hoping to see someone, something.

But there was nothing. He was all alone again, alive, but floating into nothingness, with no land in sight.

*

Gwen remained at the bow of her ship, even as it turned around, unable to pull herself away. She did not know that Thor was out there, that was true, and yet, somehow, heading south back toward where they had last seen the Empire fleet had made her feel better, as if she were getting closer to where she had last seen him. Maybe all the others had been right: maybe Thor was not there at all. Maybe, even, she hated to think, he was dead.

But as they sailed away, Gwen could not ignore her inner instinct, could not ignore that small, irrational part of herself that insisted that Thor was alive, that he was out there, that he was waiting for her. She felt as if she were leaving the last great thing in her life behind. It made no rational sense, but something inside was screaming at her, telling her that she was making a mistake.

It was telling her to turn around.

Gwendolyn, the only person left still facing the rear, standing there, clutching the baby, watched the debris bobbing in the waters. There was no sign of Thor anywhere, only black clouds looming on the horizon, getting closer and closer, and the endless ruins of what had once been the Empire fleet. Still, she realized, sometimes she just had to follow her instinct, however crazy, and do things that made no sense.

"Turn the fleet around," Gwen suddenly commanded Steffen, surprising even herself.

Steffen stared back at her, eyes wide open in shock.

"Did I hear correctly, my lady?" he asked.

She nodded.

"But why?" Kendrick asked, coming up beside her, concern etched across his face.

"I cannot turn my back on Thorgrin," Gwen said. "I sense that he's out there. I sense that he needs me."

All the others were now standing beside her, looking at her as if she were mad.

"Our people are desperate, my lady," Kendrick said. "We may not find land for who knows how long. If we turn back for Thor, who might not even be there, then we might all die trying."

Gwen faced him, her expression hard.

"Then we shall die trying."

Kendrick lowered his head, silent.

"Anyone who wants to leave us," Gwen said, her voice booming, "can join the other ships and leave us. I am turning this ship around."

Her men all stared at her, silent, in shock, then finally they broke into action.

"Turn her around!" one sailor called out.

His called was echoed up and down the line, and soon sails were hoisted, and turned, and Gwen felt the huge ship turning back around. She immediately felt better as it did, felt a rock lift from her heart.

"My sister, I am glad you trusted your instinct," Reece said. "Even if you're wrong, I admire you for it. I wanted to turn around myself."

"As did I," Kendrick added.

"And I," came the chorus of voices.

Gwen felt warmed by their support, and they all turned back to the rail and searched the waters. As Gwen stared, she heard a screech, high up, and she craned her neck and saw a familiar bird. There was Estopheles, soaring high. She screeched, swooping down then up again; Gwen felt she was trying to tell them something.

"Follow the falcon!" Gwen yelled out.

The men changed course and followed Estopheles as she led them in a different direction, through the sea of debris, their hull clacking against all the wood.

Gwen kept her eyes fixated on the water, searching everywhere, following her heart. She closed her eyes.

*Please, God. Bring him to me.*

Estopheles screeched, and Gwen watched as she dove down in the distance and landed on the ocean, behind a huge pile of debris. Gwen lost sight of her.

The ship sailed for her, and as Gwen watched the waters, suddenly, she spied something.

"There!" Gwen yelled, pointing to what looked like a body.

They sailed closer, and Gwen's heart stopped as she saw the unmistakable sight of a body draped over a pile of wood. The body floated there, and seemed cold, stiff, perhaps even lifeless. She was afraid to hope, and yet, as they got closer, the body shifted in the current and Gwen for the first time got a look at his face.

She burst into tears: there lay Thorgrin, unconscious, drifting. Gwendolyn's heart raced; she could hardly believe it. She had been right—it was really him.

"Lower the ropes!" called out a voice.

Gwen turned and handed the baby to Illepra beside her, then was the first to rush forward, grab a thick rope, and cast it overboard as they approached. Gwen didn't wait for the others, but jumped overboard herself, grabbing onto the rope and lowering herself down.

Gwen's heart pounded as she got closer, praying that Thor was alive. She reached him and jumped off the rope, into the water, landing by Thor's side.

"My lady!" someone called from above, and several men scurried down the rope to help.

Gwen ignored them; she swam up beside Thor, and grabbed him, shaking him. She saw he was unconscious, his lips blue. But he was breathing.

"He's alive!" she cried out with joy.

She wept, so relieved, hugging his limp body, clutching him, not wanting to let go. He was alive. He was really alive.

# CHAPTER FIFTEEN

Thor opened his eyes to find himself lying on his back in a rocking ship, in a dim cabin below, sunlight streaking through the slats. He felt rested for the first time in as long as he could remember, felt as if he had slept a thousand years. He felt a presence in the room before he saw it, and he squinted and looked up, and in the dim light he was overcome with joy to see a smiling face looking down on him, as a woman reached out and held his hand with the softest touch he'd ever felt. Her face so filled with love, her eyes glistening with tears, at first Thor wondered if it was just another dream.

But as he sat up, his heart lifted to realize it was not. There, before him, was the love of his life, the woman he had prayed, time and again, that he'd have one more chance to see.

Gwendolyn.

Gwen leaned in and hugged him, crying over his shoulder, and he hugged her tight. It felt surreal to hold her in his arms again. Every wish, every prayer he'd ever had, had come true. He held her tight as she cried, never wanting to let her go. He could not believe that they were together again, after all they had been through.

"You don't know how long I've wished and waited for this moment," she said into his ear, between her tears.

"I've thought of nothing but you," he replied.

"I did not think you'd ever come back to me," she said. "I only dared to dream."

Gwen pulled back and looked into his eyes. She laid her palms on his cheeks, and leaned in and kissed him, and he kissed her back, loving the feel of her lips on his. They held the kiss for such a long time, and all of Thor's memories of Gwendolyn came rushing back to him—the first time they'd met…their courtship…Guwayne's birth. Thor had never imagined loving anyone as much as her, and being here with her made him feel as if he were meeting her again for the first time.

Thor also felt a new strength within him, felt himself healed from all his wounds, rejuvenated, back to himself. He had rested and recovered on this ship, and he realized that once again, his life had been saved by Gwendolyn. He leaned back and looked her into her eyes.

"How did you find me?" he asked.

She smiled.

"It was easy," she said. "You were floating in the sea. You were hard to miss."

Thor smiled and shook his head, taking it all in.

"If you hadn't come back for me, I would be dead."

Gwendolyn smiled at him.

"And if I hadn't come back for you, I myself would have died," she replied.

She embraced him again, and he held her tight. It felt surreal to feel her in the flesh, to smell her scent, to feel the fabric of her clothes. For so long she'd been a fantasy in his mind, and he didn't know if he would ever return to her.

Thor was suddenly struck by another thought.

"And Guwayne?" he asked.

He felt Gwen tightening up in his arms, and she pulled back, and his heart fell as he saw her face become drawn, pained, her eyes downcast.

She did not reply, but instead slowly and sadly shook her head, tears dripping down her face,

"What has happened?" Thor asked, worried.

Gwen burst into tears, crying for a long time, and Thor did not know what to say. His heart was pounding as he waited for her response. Was his son alive?

"The island was under attack," Gwen finally managed to say between tears. "I was certain we would all die. I wanted to spare Guwayne our fate. So I sent him alone, into the sea. In his own boat."

Thor gasped, shocked, as Gwen wept.

"I'm so sorry," she said. "So, so sorry."

Thor leaned in and hugged her, holding her tight, rocking her, reassuring her.

"You did what was right," he said. "You cannot punish yourself. It was indeed likely you would have died—as many of our people have died."

Gwendolyn slowly calmed, and stared into his eyes.

"We must find him," she said. "I will find him or die trying."

Thor nodded in understanding.

"He will return to us," he said. "What is ours cannot be taken from us."

Gwen searched Thor's eyes with a glimmer of hope.

"Mycoples?" she asked, tentative. "Ralibar? Can they help?"

It was Thor's turn to shake his head sadly.

"I'm sorry, my love," he said. "I alone survived."

Fresh tears rolled down her face, but she nodded, stoic.

"I sensed as much," she said. "I could feel it, in my heart, in my dreams. I could feel Ralibar trying to talk to me. I loved them dearly."

"So did I," Thorgrin said.

A long silence fell over the room, as they both stared into space, lost in memories, lost in sorrow.

"And then how shall we find Guwayne, without a dragon to comb the seas?" Gwen asked.

Thor thought for a moment, reflecting, and a new purpose arose within him. He recalled his mother's words, and he sensed that what lay ahead of him would be the greatest quest of his life. It would be a quest of greater importance than his search for the Destiny Sword, greater even than his search for his mother. It would be more important than his own life itself.

"I shall find him," Thor said. "Without the aid of a dragon. Without the aid of anyone but myself. I will take a boat, and I will embark to search for him right away."

"I already tried," Gwen said, shaking her head. "I feel certain he headed north. There is no land there, nothing on any map. To lead our people there would be to kill them all. They need provisions desperately. I tried it once, and I cannot do it again."

"I understand," Thor answered. "But I can."

Gwen looked at him, hope rising in her eyes.

"You lead our people to a new land, to safety. Wherever that may be. And I shall find Guwayne."

Gwen looked pained again.

"I hate the thought of parting from you again. Not for anything," she said. "But for our son...it must be done."

They both looked at each other and came to a silent agreement to part ways, and Gwen reached out and took his hand. They stood and faced each other.

"Are you ready to greet our people?" she asked.

Gwen led him up the stairs from the cabin, and Thor squinted at the harsh daylight as they came above board.

Thor was surprised to see hundreds of his fellow people waiting there to greet him, looking at him like a hero risen from the ashes. Thor saw in their eyes such love and admiration, as if they were witnessing the emergence of a God.

They all rushed forward, and Thor embraced them, one after the next, his heart swelling with joy to see all his old friends and people again. There came Reece, then Elden, O'Connor, Conven, Kendrick, Godfrey…one face after another whom he recognized, all men whom he thought he would never see again.

"My time is short here," Thor boomed out to the crowd, as they settled down in silence. All eyes fixed on him, riveted. "I must leave you all. I go to seek out my son. I shall take one of the small boats from the rear of the ship. It will be a desolate and joyless journey, and I do not expect any of you to join me. I shall return when I find him, and not before."

In the long silence that followed, Reece stepped forward, his boots creaking on the wood, and faced Thor.

"Wherever you go, I go," Reece said. "Legion forever."

Reece was joined by Elden, O'Connor, and Conven.

"Legion forever," they echoed.

Thor looked back at them all, touched, honored to know them.

"It is a quest from which I may never return," he warned.

Reece grinned back.

"Even more reason to join it," he said.

Thor smiled back, seeing the determination on their faces, knowing he would not change their minds, and welcoming their companionship again.

"Very well then," he said. "Prepare yourselves. We shall leave at once."

*

Reece paced back and forth on the ship, gathering his few possessions, mostly weapons, and stuffed them into a sack, preparing for the journey ahead. He was elated that his best friend Thorgrin was alive, was thrilled to have him back again, and was excited to be heading out on a quest with him again. This quest, more than all the others, hit home for Reece, as they were not just searching for a weapon, but for Guwayne, his nephew. Reece could think of no two people he loved more than Gwendolyn and Thorgrin, and he could imagine no higher cause than striving to retrieve their son.

Reece prepared his weapons carefully, sharpening his sword, checking the aim on his bow, adjusting his arrows as he strapped one bow over his shoulder and another sword over his back. Reece felt that this would be the most important mission of his life, and he wanted to be prepared.

Reece tried not to think of the others he was leaving behind— Gwendolyn, Kendrick and the rest of his people, and most of all Stara; yet he felt confident he would meet up with them again, and more importantly, return victorious, with Guwayne in tow.

After all, Reece and Thorgrin were brothers of the Legion, and for Reece, that was more sacred than blood—more sacred than anything in this world. They held a bond of honor: if one of them was in trouble, all of them were in trouble. If Gwendolyn's son was missing, it was as if Reece's own son was missing. Reece recalled Kolk's words, hammered into him during training: *Don't ever imagine that you fight alone. When one of you is hurt, all of you are hurt. If you can't learn to be there for your brothers, you shall never learn to become a warrior at all. Battle is about sacrifice. The sooner you learn that, the greater warrior you will be.*

Reece regretted only one thing about this quest, and that was Stara. Although he would not admit to himself that he had feelings for her, he had to admit, at least, that he would think of her. There was something about being around her, he had to admit, that was addicting. It wasn't so much that he ached to be in her presence, but rather that, when she wasn't around, he felt her absence. Like something about him was a little bit off.

But Reece shook these thoughts away; in the forefront of his mind there still remained Selese, his mourning for her, his penitence. And sailing with Thorgrin, going on this journey, would help give

Reece time to reflect, to keep fresh his guilt for Selese. That was what he wanted.

And yet, he had to admit, there remained a part of him that felt he was abandoning Stara, even if she were here on the ship with all the others.

"So are you just going to leave then?" came a voice.

The hair stood up on Reece's back, as he heard the voice of the very person he had been thinking about—as if it were his own conscience speaking to himself.

Reece put his sword in his scabbard, turned around, and saw Stara facing him, a look of sadness and disappointment etched across her face.

Reece cleared his throat and tried to put on his bravest face.

"My brother has summoned me in his time of need," Reece replied, matter-of-factly. "What choice do I have?"

"What choice?" Stara repeated. "You have any choice you wish. You needn't go on this mission."

"Thor needs me," Reece replied.

Stara frowned.

"Thor is a great warrior. He does not need you. He does not need any of you. He can find his son on his own."

It was Reece's turn to frown.

"So then I should just leave him to the fates, whatever should happen?"

Stara looked away.

"I do not want you to go," she said. "I want you here. With me. With all of us on this ship, wherever it is that we are going. Don't I count, too? Is Thor more important than me?"

Reece looked at her, baffled. He didn't know where this was coming from; she was acting as if they were a couple—but they were not. For most of the trip, in fact, she had barely acknowledged him. Wasn't it Stara, after all, who had said they would never be together, except in mourning for Selese?

Reece was certain he would never understand the ways of women. He stepped forward and spoke softly, filled with compassion for her.

"Stara," he said, "you've been a great friend to me. But as you yourself have stated, there can no longer be anything between us. We both live together in the presence of a ghost, are both joined by mourning."

Reece sighed.

"I admit, I will miss you. I would like to be with you, in whatever way we can. But I'm sorry; my brothers need me. And when I am needed by my brother, I go. That is who I am. There is no choice there for me."

Stara looked back at him, her glowing blue eyes filled with tears, and that look haunted Reece; it was a look, he knew, that he should not easily forget.

"Go then!" she shouted.

Stara turned on her heel and stormed away. She weaved in and out of the crowd on the ship, and Reece lost sight of her, before he could even attempt to console her.

But he knew there was no consoling her. Their relationship was what it was. Reece didn't fully understand it—but then again, he was not sure that he ever would.

*

Gwendolyn stood in the center of the ship amidst all of her advisors, the entire ship huddled together as they all debated where to sail next. The conversation was exhausting and intense, going around in circles, each with his own strong opinion. Gwen had asked Thorgrin to stay for it before he embarked, and he stood beside her, with the Legion, listening in. She was grateful that he was still here and hadn't left yet. This decision was too important; she wanted him by her side. And most of all, she wanted to savor every moment with him before he left her side again.

"We cannot return to the Ring," Kendrick said, arguing with one of the people in the crowd. "It is destroyed. It would take generations to rebuild. And it is occupied."

"Nor can we return to the Upper Isles," Aberthol chimed in. "There was little there for us before the dragons destroyed it, and now there is nothing there for us."

The group grumbled with discontent, and there came a long, agitated murmur.

"Where else, then?" someone else yelled out. "Where else can we go?"

"Our provisions run too low!" another yelled. "And our maps show no isles, no land, nothing anywhere near us!"

"We shall die here on these ships!" another yelled.

Again, there came a long murmur, her people ever more agitated.

Gwendolyn shared their frustration, and she sympathized with them; she looked out to the horizon and was wondering the same thing. An endless sea lay before them, and she had no idea where to lead her people.

Suddenly, Sandara stepped forward, into the center of the crowd, so tall and beautiful and noble and exotic, with her dark skin and glowing yellow eyes and her commanding presence; she was a proud and graceful woman who commanded attention, and all eyes turned to her. The crowd grew silent as she faced Gwendolyn.

"You can go to my people," she said.

Gwen stared back at her in shock, and the silence deepened.

"Your people?" Gwen asked.

Sandara nodded.

"They will take you in. I will see to it."

Gwen looked back, confused.

"And where are your people?" she asked.

"They inhabit a remote province. Outside the city of Volusia. The capital of the Northern region of the Empire."

"The Empire?" someone in the crowd yelled out in outrage, and there came a long, upset murmur from the crowd.

"Would you have us all sail into the heart of the Empire?" a man called out.

"Would you lead a lamb to slaughter?" another yelled.

"Why not just surrender us to Romulus? Why not just kill us all right here?" another called out.

Increasing murmurs of discontent arose from the crowd, until Kendrick finally stepped up to Sandara's side, and protective of her, yelled out for silence, banging a staff on the deck.

The crowd finally quieted, and Gwendolyn, not sure what to make of it all, faced Sandara. She knew her options were dim, but this seemed insane.

"Explain yourself," Gwen commanded.

"You do not understand the Empire," Sandara said, "because you have never been there. It is my homeland. The Empire is more vast than you can imagine, and it is fractured. Not all provinces think alike. There is inner conflict amongst them. It is a fragile alliance. The Empire was formed by the conquering of one people after the next, and the discontent amongst the conquered runs deep.

"The Empire's lands are so vast, there are places that remain hidden. Separatist regions. Yes, they have subjugated all of our free people, have made us all slaves. But there are still places, if you know where to look, where you can hide. My people will hide you. They have food and shelter. You can make land there, hide there, recover there, and then decide where you should go next."

A long silence fell over the ship.

"What we need is a new home, not a place for shelter," Aberthol pointed out, his voice old, strained.

"Perhaps it shall become a home," Godfrey said.

"A home? In the Empire? In the lap of our enemy?" Srog said.

"What other choice do we have?" Brandt said. "The Ring was the last unoccupied territory of the Empire. Anywhere we go will be Empire."

"And what of the Southern Isles?" Atme called out. "And Erec?"

Kendrick shook his head.

"We could never reach them. We are too far north. We don't have provisions enough. And even if we did, we'd have to pass too close to the currents of the Ring, and we'd have to fight Romulus's men."

"There must be some other place for us!" a man called out.

The crowd broke into more shouts of discontent, arguing with each other.

Gwendolyn stood there, holding Thor's hand, and she pondered Sandara's words. The more she considered it, as crazy as it was, the more she liked the idea.

She raised a palm, and slowly, the crowd quieted.

"The Empire will be combing the seas, searching for us," Gwen said. "It will only be a matter of time until they hunt us down. But the last place they would look for us would be within the Empire, within their very own regions, and close to one of their capitals. Romulus has millions of men, and they will search the earth for us, and eventually they will find us. We need a new home, that is true, but right now, what we need above all, is a safe harbor. Fresh provisions. Shelter. And sailing right into the Empire would be the most counterintuitive move they could expect. Perhaps, paradoxically, we would be safest there."

The crowd quieted, looking back at Gwendolyn with respect, and she turned to Sandara. Gwen saw honesty and intelligence in her beautiful face, and she felt comfortable with her. Her brother loved her, and that was enough for Gwendolyn.

"You may lead us to your home," Gwendolyn said. "It is a sacred task, leading a people. We are putting ourselves at your mercy."

Sandara nodded solemnly.

"And lead you there, I shall," she replied. "I vow it. If I have to die trying."

Gwendolyn nodded back, satisfied.

"It is done!" Gwen called out. "To the Empire we sail!"

There came more agitated mumbling on deck, but also many shouts of excitement and approval, as her people immediately began to set sails for a new course.

An angry citizen came up to Gwendolyn.

"You better hope your plan works," he scowled. "We have three ships, remember, and those of us who don't agree can take one and leave you anytime we wish."

Gwen reddened, indignant.

"You speak treason," Thor growled, stepping forward, close to the man, hand on his sword.

Gwen reached out and laid a reassuring hand on his, and Thor softened.

"And where will you go?" Gwen asked the man calmly.

The citizen glared.

"Anywhere that is a place of common sense," he snapped, and turned and stormed off.

Gwen turned and exchanged a look with Thor. She was so happy he was still here, taking solace in his presence.

Thor shook his head.

"That was a bold decision," he said. "I admire it greatly. And your father would have, too."

Thor prepared to embark, his Legion members standing near the small boat waiting to be lowered, and Gwen reached out and laid a hand on his wrist.

He turned to her.

"Before you go," she said, I want you to meet someone.

Gwen nodded, and Illepra stepped forward and handed her the baby she had rescued on the Upper Isles.

Gwen held the child up to Thor, who looked back, eyes wide in surprise.

"You saved her life," Gwen said softly. "You appeared just in time. Your fate is linked with hers; as is mine. Her parents are dead; we are all she has. She is Guwayne's age. Their fates are linked, too. I can feel it."

Thor's eyes welled up as he examined her.

"She is beautiful," he said.

"I cannot let her go," Gwen said.

"Nor should you," Thor replied.

Gwen nodded, satisfied that Thor felt as she.

"I know you must go," Gwen said. "But before you do, you must get a blessing. From Argon."

Thor looked back at her in surprise.

"Argon?" he said. "Has he awoken?"

Gwendolyn shook her head.

"He has not spoken since the Upper Isles. He's not dead, but he's not alive either. Maybe for you, he would come back."

They walked across the ship, to the very end, until they came to Argon. He lay there, surrounded by her guards, on a stack of furs, hands across his chest, eyes closed.

Gwen and Thor knelt by his side, and it broke Gwen's heart to see him in this state—especially since his sacrifice for all of them had led him here.

They each rested a hand on Argon's shoulder as they knelt there, watching him patiently.

"Argon?" Gwen asked softly.

They waited, feeling the rocking of the waves. Gwen knew they could not wait much longer; Guwayne was out there, after all.

Finally, after what seemed like an eternity, Thor turned to her.

"I cannot wait," he said.

Gwen nodded, understanding.

As Thor began to rise, suddenly Gwen reached out and grabbed his wrist and pointed: Argon had opened his eyes.

Thor knelt back down, and Argon stared right at him. He nodded his head, and it seemed to be in approval.

"Argon," Thor said, "give me a blessing."

"You have it," he whispered, laying a hand on Thor's wrist. "But you don't need it. You will create your own blessings."

"Argon, tell me," Gwen said, "is our son alive? Will we find him? Will you bless us to find him?"

Argon closed his eyes and shook his head, withdrawing his hand.

"I cannot alter what is predestined," he said.

Gwen felt a pit in her stomach at his words, and she and Thor exchanged a concerned look.

"Will we reach the Empire?" Gwen asked. "Will we live?"

Argon was silent for a long time, so long, Gwen wondered if he would ever reply. Just as they were preparing to leave, he reached out and grabbed her wrist. He stared at her with such intensity, his eyes shining, that she nearly had to look away.

"On the far side of the world, in the Empire, I see another great warrior, a young man rising up. If he lives, and if you reach him, together, you may achieve what no one else can."

"Who is this young man?" Gwen pressed.

But Argon closed his eyes, and after a long while, she realized he had gone back to his state. She was left pondering, wondering. Did that mean they would make it? Did her people's fate really depend on a single boy? And most of all: who was he?

# CHAPTER SIXTEEN

Darius grunted as he swung the blunt ax high and brought it down in a high arc, over his shoulder, onto a large, green boulder. It smashed before him into a pile of small rocks, green dust rising up in a cloud, covering him, as it had since the sunrise. The pungent smell of athox burned his nose, and he tried to turn his head.

Darius knew it would do him little good: he was mired in the dust from head to toe, after another long day of labor, as he had been nearly every day of his life. At fifteen years of age, his hands were raw, his clothing tattered, having spent nearly all his life in labor, in hard, backbreaking work. It was the life of a slave and, like all of his people, he hardly knew anything different.

But Darius dreamed of a different life, even if it was a life he never knew. He looked like his people, with his brown skin, his yellow eyes, and his muscular frame; but there was something about him that set him apart. With his proud, noble jaw, glistening eyes, and broad forehead, he did not carry himself like a slave, as many of his people did; instead, he had the heart and soul of a warrior. He exuded courage and honor, pride, and a refusal to be broken. And while all of his people had short hair, Darius's was long and curly, brown, wild, untamed, pulled back in a long ponytail and dangling behind his back. It was his mark of individuality in a subjugated world, and he refused to cut it. More than once his friends had taunted him for it—yet after too many times of Darius challenging them and proving himself a better fighter, the taunts finally stopped and they learned to live with his uniqueness.

With not an ounce of fat on his rippling body, Darius, even though he was not as muscular as some of the others, was stronger and quicker than nearly all of them. He was, he felt—he had always felt—different from his people, destined to be a great warrior. Destined to be free.

Yet as Darius looked around, he saw how different reality was from the destiny he imagined for himself. Day in and day out, he was a slave, like all of his people, a subject for the Empire to do with as they wished. Darius knew his people were not alone: the Empire had enslaved all peoples, of all color skin and eyes, in all the lands of the world. They had enslaved anyone who was not of their race, anyone who did not have the glowing yellow skin of the elite Empire race, who did not have the two small horns behind their ears, the long pointed ears, the extra height and breadth, the too-muscular bodies, and the glistening red eyes. Not to mention the fangs. The Empire believed themselves to be a master race, a superior race.

But Darius did not believe it for a second. The Empire did have superior numbers, and superior arms and organization, and they had used their brutality, their strength in numbers—and most of all, their dark sorcery—to enforce it, to subjugate others to their will. Mercy did not exist in the Empire culture; they seemed to thrive on brutality, and for every slave, there seemed to be ten Empire taskmasters. They were a race of soldiers. They were better armed, better organized, and their hundred-million-man army seemed to be everywhere at once.

It would all make sense if the Empire were barbarians—but Darius had heard of their cities, shining with gold, and had heard the Empire race was incredibly sophisticated and civilized. It was a paradox he could not reconcile in his mind, try as he did.

Darius tried to take solace where he could; at least in his region, the Empire did not kill them. He'd heard of other regions where the Empire did not even keep people alive to be slaves, but rather sold them off to slave markets, split them from their families, or just spent the days torturing and killing them. He had heard of yet other places where they starved the slaves, feeding them once a week, and of still others where they beat the slaves so bad, all day long, that few of them even reached Darius's age.

At least here, in Darius's province, outside the great Northern Empire city of Volusia, they had come to a cold agreement with the Empire, where the Empire kept them as slaves, but did not beat them often, allowed them to eat, and allowed them to live. And at least when Darius's people retreated to their own village at night, they were far enough away from the prying eyes of the Empire to build up their own, secret resistance. When the day of labor ended, they gathered and trained; they became better warriors, and slowly but surely, they gathered weapons. They were crude weapons, not iron or steel like the

Empire, but still weapons all the same. They were slowly preparing, in Darius's mind at least, for a great uprising.

Yet it frustrated Darius to no end that others did not see it that way. Darius smashed another boulder, wiping sweat from his brow, and grimaced. His fellow villagers, especially the older ones, were all too safe, too conservative. They had talked of uprising Darius's entire life, and yet no one ever took any action. All they did was train and train to become better warriors—and yet no one ever acted on it.

Darius was reaching a breaking point inside. He'd allowed himself to maintain his pride, despite his situation, all his life, because he lived for the day of uprising, for the day of asserting his freedom. And yet, increasingly, as he watched others settle into a life of apathy, his fears grew that that day would never come. Darius smashed yet another rock, wondering if all this training might just be a way for the elders to keep them down, to keep them occupied, to give them hope. And to keep them in their place.

Yes, perhaps they had it better than most, but even so, this still was not a life. He had seen too many of his cousins die from random acts of cruelty, had been lashed himself one too many times, to ever forgive or forget. Darius loathed the Empire with everything he had. He wouldn't just lie down like the elders and accept life for what it was. Darius felt that he was different from the others, that he had less of a tolerance for it, less willingness to accept it. He knew deep down inside that he could not continue to wait for the elders much longer. Eventually, if no one else acted, he would, even if it led to his own death. Better to die struggling to be a free man, Darius felt, than to live a long life as a slave to someone else.

Darius looked around him at the hundred or so boys in this field of green dust, all of them smashing rocks, all of them covered in the dust that had come to mark their identities. Some of them were his close friends, others were family members; still others were boys that he trained with, muscular boys, most of them larger and bigger than he, and older, some sixteen, seventeen, eighteen, and some even in their twenties. Darius was one of the youngest and smallest of the bunch—and yet he held his own, fought as hard as any of them. They respected his skills, and they accepted him, though they tested him often.

Darius also had something else that none of the others had—something he had kept a secret his entire life, determined to never let anyone else know of. It was a power, a power he did not understand. His people scorned sorcery and magic of all sorts; it was strictly forbidden, and it had been ingrained into him since he was a child. It was ironic, Darius thought, because his village was rife with seers and prophets and healers who used mystical arts. Yet when it came to sorcery in battle, it was considered a disgrace. They would all rather die as slaves at the hand of the Empire.

So Darius had kept it close to himself, knowing he would be an outcast if it was discovered. He also, he had to admit, was afraid of it himself. He had been shocked the day he had stumbled upon it, just recently, and he still was unsure if his power was real, or if it had just been a fluke. He had been pushing back a rock, preparing to smash it with his ax, and he had unearthed a nest of scorpions. One of them had made for his ankle, a jumping scorpion, black with yellow stripes, the most lethal of all, and Darius knew that the second it touched his skin, he'd be dead.

Darius had not even thought—he had just reacted. He had pointed his finger toward it, and a light, so fast, like a flash, had shot forth. The insect had flown backwards, several feet, landing on its back, dead.

Darius had been more scared of the discovery of his power than he had been of the scorpion. He had looked all around to make sure no one had seen him, and luckily no one had. He did not know what they would think of him if they had. Would they consider him a freak?

Darius suspected that, deep down, his people did not really scorn magic; he guessed that the real fear of the elders was that the Empire would find out. The Empire had a scorched-earth policy for anyone discovered with any sort of magic powers. When people from other towns were discovered or suspected to have powers, the Empire had come in and devastated the entire town, murdered every last single man, woman, and child. Perhaps, Darius thought, the elders frowned upon it so much out of self-preservation. Secretly, of course, they would love to have powers that could topple the Empire. How could they not?

Darius tried to focus on his work, smashing rock twice as hard, trying to block these thoughts from his mind. He knew they were not useful. This was his lot, at least for now. Until he was prepared to do something about it, he had to suppress his feelings.

There came a sudden rumbling, followed by distant screams. Darius stopped and turned with all the others, the air falling silent for the first time that day, as they all examined the horizon. It was a familiar sound: the sound of a collapse. Darius looked to the red mountains looming over them in the distance, where thousands of his people worked, those less fortunate, who had been assigned to till underneath the earth, mining inside the caves. It was hot here, even for Darius, and they all worked with no shirts under the beating sun of the Empire, on these hard red sands; but up there, on the mountain ridges, underneath the earth, it was even hotter. Too hot. Hot enough to cause the weak soil of the ridges to give way. Darius's heart fell as he watched the final crumbling of a mountain ridge, and saw dozens of Empire guards shouting as they plummeted into the earth.

The two Empire taskmasters watching over Darius's group, donned in the finest armor and weaponry of the sharpest steel, both turned to the horizon with alarm. They broke into a run, as the Empire often did when one of their own was injured or killed. They left them alone—yet, of course, they knew that the slaves would not dare run. They had nowhere to go, and if they tried, they would be hunted down and killed—and their entire families killed as retribution.

Darius saw his friends shake their heads grimly at the sight, all pausing from their work, studying the horizon with grave concern. Darius knew they were all thinking the same thing: they were lucky they hadn't been the ones picked to mine underground today. They looked weighed down by guilt, and Darius wondered how many of them had friends of family trapped or dying up there. It had somehow become a way of life, being immune to the deaths that happened here every day, as if all of this was normal. Death tainted the air here in these arid lands, in these rolling deserts and mountains swept by heat and dust. *A land of fire*, his grandfather called it.

"I hope it took out more Empire than us," one of the boys called out.

They all leaned on their axes, and if nothing else, Darius thought, at least this would give them a break. After all, the taskmasters would not return for several hours, given how far away those mountain ridges were.

"I don't know about you," came a deep voice, "but I think those are two fine-looking zertas."

Darius recognized his friend Raj's voice, and he turned and followed his glance and saw what he was looking at: there sat two Empire zertas, large, proud, beautiful animals, all white, twice the size of horses, looking much like horses, but taller, wider, with thick skin, almost like armor, and instead of a mane, having long, sloping yellow horns that began behind their ears. They were glorious animals, and these two, tied up beneath a tree in the shade, chewing on the grass, were the most beautiful Darius had ever seen.

Darius could see mischief in Raj's eyes as he examined them.

"I don't know about the rest of you," Raj added, "but I don't intend to stand here all day and wait for their return. I want a break—and I think those zertas can use a ride."

"Are you crazy?" one of the other boys said. "Those belong to the Empire. They catch you leaving here, they'll kill you. They catch you on their zertas, they'll probably torture your entire family, after they torture you first."

Raj shrugged, leaned back, and wiped his palms on his pants.

"They might," he said, then grinned, "but then again, they might not. And like you said, they have to catch me."

Raj turned and studied the horizon.

"I doubt they'll beat me back. They'll never even know their precious animals were gone. Any of you want to come?"

Darius was hardly surprised; Raj had always been the daredevil of the bunch, fearless, proud, boastful, and the first to incite others. All qualities Darius admired, except Raj was reckless, too, and lacked good judgment.

But Darius shared his restlessness, and he could hardly blame him. Indeed, at Raj's words, there welled up within Darius a fierce desire to go, to let loose, to stop being so cautious as he had always been. He, too, wanted to stop laboring, wanted to get out of this place. He would love to go on a ride, to take an adventure on that zerta, and see where it took him. To have fun for one day in his life. To have just a small taste of freedom.

"Is there not one of you who has the courage to join me?" Raj asked. He was taller than the other boys, older, with broader shoulders, and he slowly scanned the crowd, looking at all of them with disdain. All the boys turned away, shook their heads, looked down to the ground.

"It's not worth it," one boy said. "I have a family. I have a life."

"Maybe this moment is your life," Raj countered.

But all the boys looked away, not saying a word.

"I'll join you," Darius heard himself say, his voice deep, distinct, powerful beyond his fifteen years, reverberating in his chest.

All the boys in the group turned and looked at Darius in shock, and Raj stared at him too, clearly surprised. Slowly, a smile crossed his face, along with a look of admiration. His smile broadened to one of mischief.

"I knew there was something about you that I liked," Raj said.

*

Darius and Raj rode side by side on the zertas, laughing aloud as the beasts galloped through the winding paths of the Alluvian Forest, the wind in Darius's hair, blowing back his ponytail, taking the heat off his neck, cooling down the hot day and making him feel free for the first time in years. This was reckless, he knew, and might even get him killed—but a part of him no longer cared. At least for now, in this moment, he was free.

Darius hadn't ventured into the Alluvian Forest in years, yet he had never forgotten it. A broad dirt path cut down its center, and above them a canopy of trees arched low overhead, so low that sometimes they had to duck. The forest was famous for its light green leaves, so light they were nearly translucent, glistening and shimmering in the sun above and casting a beautiful light down on the path. It was a sight that Darius had never forgotten, and even seeing it again now took his breath away. The trees, too, were unique, their bark nearly translucent, expanding and contracting all the time, as if they were breathing, and the forest had a unique sound, a soft rustling sound as the leaves swayed, almost like a grove of bamboo.

It was a magical place, Darius felt, a place of true beauty in the midst of this arid landscape. As he raced, he felt the sweat perpetually caked on his brow beginning to dissipate.

"Not as fast as your elders, are you?" Raj called out, teasing, and suddenly took the lead, heading out several feet in front of Darius.

Darius kicked his zerta, catching up to him. Then Darius took the lead and leapt boldly over a felled trunk of an ancient tree. Now it was his turn to laugh.

Soon enough the two were back to riding side-by-side, and as they galloped deeper into the forest, Darius had never felt so free, so liberated. It was unlike him, he who had been so cautious his whole life, who had always planned everything perfectly; for once, he let himself go. For once, he gave into the recklessness, not knowing where they were going, and not caring. As long as they were out from under the taskmasters' eyes, and as long as they were choosing their own path.

"You know if we get caught we'll get flogged for this, don't you?" Darius called out.

Raj smiled back.

"And what is life without a good flogging every now and again?" he called back.

Darius grinned as Raj galloped out front and took the lead. Darius then caught up and took the lead himself.

"I'll race you!" Raj called out.

"Race me to where!?" Darius replied.

Raj laughed. "Who cares! Nowhere! As long as I am first!"

Raj laughed and took the lead, but then Darius caught up to him. The two raced, each alternately taking the lead, back and forth, competing with each other, each gaining the edge then losing it. They stood on the saddles as they rode, wearing broad smiles, the wind blowing in their faces. Darius relished the feel of the shade; if nothing else, it felt so good be out of the sun, and it felt ten degrees cooler here in the forest.

They turned a bend, and Darius spotted, at the end of the path, a wall of dangling red vines. It demarcated the forbidden zone.

Darius suddenly got nervous, knowing they had reached the limit to where they could go. No one crossed the vines—that was Empire territory. The only slaves allowed outside were the women, and only in their labor. If they crossed as men, they'd be killed on the spot.

"The vines!" Darius called to Raj. "We must turn back!"

Raj shook his head.

"Let us ride. As boys. As warriors. As men," he called out.

Raj turned to him, and added: "Unless, of course, you are afraid."

Raj did not wait for a response, but screamed, kicked his beast, and rode faster, heading right for the red wall of vines. Darius, his heart pounding, his face flush from the indignity, felt that Raj was going too far. Yet at the same time, he could not turn around. Not after being challenged.

Darius kicked his horse and caught up to Raj, and Raj grinned to see him at his side.

"You are growing on me," Raj said. "I see you are as stupid as I!"

They both ducked their heads and, together, they rode through the wall of vines.

As they burst through to the other side, Darius looked around, shocked. It was his first time on this side of the Alluvian Forest, and here everything was different. The trees changed color, from green to red, and he saw that the path, in the distance, led out to a clearing demarcated by a thick canopy of red trees. He looked up and saw swinging vines overhead, and saw strange animals swinging from branches; their exotic shrieks pierced the air.

They rode until they reached the very edge of the Alluvian, and they both stopped, breathing hard, their zertas winded, too, and sat there, side-by-side, looking out at the clearing.

Darius saw before him a dozen women from his village, working the wells, each pumping the long iron rods, filling water for pails. The women all labored hard, with humility, heads down, hands raw from the pumping.

On the outskirts of the clearing stood several Empire soldiers, standing guard.

"See anyone you like?" Raj asked, with a mischievous smile.

Darius shook his head, his anxiety increasing at the sight of the guards.

"We shouldn't be here," Darius said. "We should turn back. We have gone far enough. Too far. This is more than a game now."

Raj looked out, taking in all the girls, undeterred.

"I like the one with the long hair. In the back. Wearing the white dress."

Darius looked over the women, realizing Raj was not going to listen to him. He was not in the mood for this. And what bothered him even more was that he was shy around girls. And this was hardly the place or the time.

But as Darius looked them over, despite himself, there was one girl that riveted him. She had just turned from the well, and as she did, he caught a glimpse of her face, and his heart stopped. She was the most beautiful girl he'd ever seen. She was tall, well-built, looked to be about his age, with short, black hair, almond skin, and light yellow eyes. Her features were not that delicate, with a strong jaw and chin, and broad shoulders and a stocky build, but there was something about her—the shape of her eyes, the curve of her hips, the way she stood so tall, so proud—a certain dignity to her—that completely mesmerized Darius.

"Who is that?" Darius whispered to Raj. "That girl there. With the yellow dress."

"*Her?*" Raj asked disdainfully. "Why do you settle on her? She's not as pretty as the others."

Darius flushed, embarrassed.

"She is to me," he said indignantly.

Raj shrugged.

"I believe her name is Loti. My parents exchange goods with hers. She lives on the far side of the village, behind the cave mounds. She rarely comes to town. She comes from a family of warriors. Strong-willed. Not an easy girl to tame. Why don't you choose someone easier, prettier?"

Suddenly, a zerta charged into the clearing from the opposite side, and all the girls stopped what they were doing. Darius looked over and saw an Empire officer, wearing a uniform different than the others, ride in and come to a stop in the clearing. He slowly surveyed all the women, and they all looked back up at him with fear. All except Loti, who remained proud, expressionless.

The officer breathed hard and looked around as if he were looking for a snack, something to satisfy his urges. His roving eyes finally stopped on Loti.

Loti, balancing two pails of water over her shoulder, averted her eyes, looking away, clearly hoping he did not settle on her.

But the officer grinned an evil grin, showing his yellow fangs, his red eyes flashing as he dismounted and, spurs jingling, the dust rising beneath him, strutted directly for Loti.

He stared down at her, and she finally looked back at him, defiant.

"What, no smile for me?" he asked. "Have you slaves not learned to please your masters when they address you?"

Loti grimaced.

"I'm not your slave," she replied, "and you're not my master. You are a heathen. It doesn't matter how many slaves you trap beneath you—it will never change what you are."

The officer stared back at her, mouth agape, shocked. Clearly, he had never been spoken to that way before. Darius was shocked, too, and in awe at her courage.

The officer reached back and backhanded her across the face, and the sound shattered the silence as it tore through the clearing. Loti cried out and stumbled backwards.

As Darius watched, he had involuntary reaction; he could not restrain himself. Something shifted within him, and he suddenly lunged forward, to stop the officer.

Darius felt a strong hand on his chest, and he looked over to seek Raj next to him, holding him back, looking nervous and serious for the first time that day.

"Don't do it," he said. "Do you hear me? You'll get us killed. All of us. The girl, too."

He squeezed Darius's shirt hard, and Darius's muscles tensed up in his grip, and Darius stayed there, reluctantly, before conceding. Darius decided to wait and watch, willing to see what happened next before he took any action.

The officer turned and walked to his zerta, and Darius relaxed, assuming he was about to mount it and leave. But instead, he reached to his saddle and pulled out a long shining dagger with a copper hilt, and held it up glistening in the sun, grinning cruelly at Loti as he began to walk back toward her.

"Now you'll learn what it means to be a slave," he said.

Loti's eyes widened in defiance as she dropped the pails of water from her shoulder and faced him. To her credit, she did not back away, but continued to stare at him defiantly. Who was this girl, Darius wondered? How could she have such a strong spirit?

"You can kill me," Loti said, "but you will never claim my soul. My brothers and all the souls of my ancestors will avenge me."

The officer grimaced and, raising his dagger, rushed toward her.

Darius had to act; he knew he could not wait another moment. He shook of Raj's grasp, and as he did, he began to feel a power well up within him, a power he had felt but a few times in his life. It was like a heat, like a prickling sensation, taking over him, slowly climbing up his skin. He did not understand what it was—but right now, he did not wish to. He only wished to embrace it, to wield it.

Darius examined the clearing, and as he did, the world slowed; he was able to see every blade of grass, to hear every sound, every chirping of every insect; he felt almost as if he were able to slow time. He entered a strange dimension, where he was not really here, caught in some gap in the fabric of the universe.

His eyes focused on a small red scorpion that he had not seen before, and, using the power within him, Darius pointed a finger toward it. As he did, the scorpion suddenly lifted out of the grass and went flying across the clearing. It lodged itself onto the officer's calf. It was not a lethal scorpion, but it would suffice to hurt him badly—and incapacitate him for a while.

The officer, just feet away from Loti, suddenly screamed out and dropped to his knees, clutching the back of his calf.

"Help!" he shrieked, his voice cracking.

The Empire guards quickly ran to him, grabbing his arms, trying to drag him to his feet.

"My leg!" he shrieked.

One of the guards reached down with his dagger and sliced the scorpion from his leg, and the officer's shrieks filled the clearing.

"Get me back!" he yelled. "Now!"

They quickly mounted him on his zerta, and his zerta took off, racing through the clearing and disappearing back into the forest.

Darius quickly looked around, wondering if Raj suspected anything, and Raj looked back at him with a different look, a somber look, perhaps a look of suspicion, or of awe. But he did not say anything, and Darius did not know what he'd seen, if anything.

Raj turned to go, and as Darius turned to join him, he did notice, from the periphery of his eye, one person staring back at him with an unmistakable look of awe: he turned, and his eyes locked with Loti's. She had seen him. She knew what he did. She knew his secret.

# CHAPTER SEVENTEEN

Alistair stood against the wall of Erec's chamber, craning her neck up at the window, side-by-side with Erec's mother, and looked out the window in fear. She could see hundreds of torches, an angry mob of Southern Islanders hurrying through the night, chanting, all making their way in a procession toward the house of the sick. They were being led by Bowyer, and she knew they were coming right for her.

"The devil girl has escaped!" one of them yelled, "but we shall tear her apart with our own hands!"

"For the murder of Erec!" another cried out.

The crowd chanted and roared as they marched in procession right for her.

Erec's mother turned to her, face grave.

"Listen to me," she said urgently, clutching her wrist, "stay by my side and do as I say. You will be fine. Do you trust me?"

Alistair looked at her, her eyes welling with tears, and nodded back. She looked over her shoulder and saw Erec, fast asleep, and at least took solace in that.

"Will he be able to help us?" his mother asked.

Alistair shook her head sadly.

"The healing spell I cast on him takes a long time to take effect. He'll be sleeping. Perhaps for days. We are on our own."

His mother bore the news with the resolve of a woman who has seen it all, and she took her hand, led her across the room, opened the door to Erec's chamber, and closed it firmly behind them.

They marched down the stone corridors of the house of the sick, all the way to the barred main doors, tall wooden doors that were already buckling as the mob slammed against them.

"Let us in!" someone in the crowd yelled. "Or we shall knock it down!"

The two guards who stood before it turned and looked at Erec's mother, puzzled, clearly not knowing what to do.

"My Queen?" one asked. "What do you command?"

Erec's mother stood proudly, fearlessly, with the fearless countenance of a queen, and Alistair could see in that moment where Erec got it from.

"Open those doors," she commanded, her voice dark and hard. "We hide from no one."

"Stand back!" a guard yelled out, and he then removed the iron bars on the doors and opened them wide.

The move clearly surprised the mob; stunned, caught off guard, instead of rushing forward they stood there as the doors opened wide, staring back at the Queen and at Alistair.

"The devil girl!" one called out. "There she is, back to harm Erec again! Kill her!"

The crowd cheered and began to press forward, and Erec's mother stepped forward and held out a palm.

"You shall do nothing of the sort!" she boomed, with the commanding voice of a queen, of a woman used to being listened to.

The crowd stopped in their tracks and looked at her, clearly a woman they respected. Stepping out front and facing her was Bowyer, leading them.

"What do you mean by this?" he demanded. "Will you protect her? The woman who tried to murder your own son?"

"My son is not murdered," she replied. "He is healing. Thanks to Alistair."

The crowd mumbled, skeptical.

"Why would she heal him after she tried to kill him?" one called out.

"I do not believe he is healing. He is dead! She is just trying to protect the girl!" another yelled.

"He is healing, and he's very much alive!" Erec's mother insisted. "You shall not lay a hand on this girl. She did not try to murder him. It was not her." Erec's mother turned to Bowyer and pointed. "It was *him*!" she boomed.

The crowd gasped in shock, as all eyes turned to Bowyer. But he fixed his scowl on Alistair.

"All a lie!" he yelled back.

"Alistair, step forward," the former queen said.

The crowd quieted, now unsure, as Alistair stepped forward humbly.

"Tell them," she said.

"It is true," Alistair said. "Bowyer tried to murder him. I witnessed it with my own eyes."

The crowd gasped and grumbled, swaying with indecision.

"It is easy to accuse others after you have been caught with the murder weapon!" Bowyer called out.

The crowd broke into an agitated murmur, vacillating.

"I do not ask for you all to believe her!" Erec's mother called out. "I only request she have a chance to assert her right of truth."

She nodded, and Alistair stepped forward and said:

"I challenge you, Bowyer, to drink from the fountain of truth!"

The crowd gasped again, shocked by this turn, and they then quieted, somewhat satisfied, as all eyes turned and fixed on Bowyer.

Bowyer flushed, enraged.

"I need not accept her challenge!" he called out. "I need not accept a challenge from anyone! I am King now, and I demand she be executed!"

"You are *not* King!" Erec's mother yelled back. "Not while my son is alive! And no man in our kingdom, no honest man, can reject a challenge to drink from the stone. It is a tradition even of kings, of my father and his father before him. You know this as well as us. Accept the girl's challenge, if you've nothing to hide. Or reject it, and be imprisoned for the attempted murder of my son!"

The crowd cheered in approval as they all turned to Bowyer. He stood there, squirming, clearly on the spot, and Alistair could see the storm of emotions within him. She could see that he wanted more than anything to draw his sword and kill her. But he could not. Not with all these eyes on him.

Slowly Bowyer loosened his grip on his sword and sighed angrily.

"I accept the challenge!" he yelled.

The crowd cheered, and Bowyer turned and stormed through the crowd as it parted ways for him.

Alistair looked at Erec's mother, and she nodded back solemnly.

"It is time to reveal the truth."

*

Alistair, after ascending level after level of steps, moving with the throng, finally reached the highest plateau on the island, and she entered the small plaza to see before her an ancient stone fountain.

The fountain was immense, made of shining white marble streaked with black and yellow, and unlike anything Alistair had ever seen. On it was a large gargoyle, and through its open mouth there trickled glowing, red water. The water was caught in a basin below and circulated back in the fountain.

The crowd fell silent upon her arrival, and it slowly parted ways for her, clearing a space for her to approach. In the tense silence that followed, all that could be heard was the soft gurgling of the fountain.

Erec's mother, standing beside her, nodded to her reassuringly, and Alistair parted from the crowd and walked alone toward the fountain. Hundreds of Southern Islanders stood around it, clearing a space, and as they did, one other person stepped forward: Bowyer.

Alistair and Bowyer, standing beside each other next to the fountain, turned and faced the crowd. The plaza was lit by hundreds of torches, and in the distance, on the horizon, Alistair could see dawn slowly breaking, the southern sky lighting up, turning a pale shade of purple.

As she stood there, waiting, Bowyer scowling at her, there appeared from the crowd an old man, wearing a ceremonial yellow cloak, with a drawn, grave face. He held out before him, in both hands, a small, yellow marble bowl.

His face was somber, and he looked at Alistair and Bowyer with a grave expression.

"These are the waters of truth," he boomed out, his voice ancient, the silent crowd hanging on his every word. "Anyone telling the truth cannot be affected by them. But a liar who drinks will suffer an immediate and painful death."

The old man turned and studied Alistair sternly.

"Alistair, you stand accused of attempted murder of your husband-to-be. You claim innocence. Now is your time to prove it. You shall take this bowl and drink from the waters. If you have done what you are accused of having done, you shall die here on the spot. Do you have any final words?" he asked as he held the bowl to Alistair.

Alistair looked back at him proudly.

"They shall not be my last words," she said, "as I have nothing to hide."

The crowd watched, engrossed, as Alistair took the bowl and leaned forward over the fountain. The sound of trickling water filling her ears, she reached out, placed the bowl beneath, and captured some of the red liquid. She held the small bowl in both hands, filled with the red water, then put it to her mouth.

Alistair took a tentative taste, then she drank until she finished the entire bowl.

When she was done, she turned the bowl upside down and held it out for all to see.

Alistair stood there, feeling completely fine, and the crowd gasped, clearly shocked.

Alistair then turned and handed the bowl to Bowyer.

Bowyer stood there, scowling at her, and he looked at the bowl. She could see him trying to disguise his fear as he looked at her. Several tense moments passed, the tension in the air thick enough to cut it with a knife.

"Take the bowl!" a crowd member shouted.

"Take the bowl, take the bowl!" came a chorus of shouts, increasingly angry, as Bowyer stood there, nervous, shifting.

The crowd, irate, turned on him, yelling and heckling him, as if finally realizing that Alistair had been right.

Bowyer finally reached out—but instead of taking the bowl, he smacked it from Alistair's hands.

The crowd gasped as the sacred marble bowl fell to the ground and shattered into pieces.

"I do not need your stupid rituals!" Bowyer yelled. "This fountain is a myth! I am King, and no one else. I am the greatest fighter amongst you—if there is anyone good enough to challenge me, step forward!"

The crowd stared, shocked by the turn of events, unsure what to do.

Bowyer shouted in rage, drew his sword, and suddenly charged Alistair, raising it to bring it down to her chest.

The crowd, now indignant, broke into action and charged to stop him.

Alistair stood there fearlessly, and felt a great heat rise within her. She closed her eyes and as she did, she sensed his sword, felt it coming toward her. She used her power, deep within, to change the sword's direction.

Alistair opened her eyes and saw the sword stopped in midair; Bowyer stood there, grunting and groaning, trying to plunge it down with all his might. His hand shook from the effort, until finally the sword fell from his hands, landing on the stone plaza with a great clang.

Bowyer looked up at Alistair, and for the first time he showed fear.

"Devil woman!" he shouted.

Bowyer turned and ran across the plaza as the mob chased him. He mounted his horse, joined by a dozen of his tribesmen, and took off straight down the mountainside.

"I am King! And no one will stop me!"

As he and his men took off, the crowd gathered around Alistair, clearly apologetic and concerned for her welfare. Erec's mother came up beside her, ecstatic, and draped an arm around her shoulder. They both stood there and looked out into the breaking dawn together.

"A civil war is coming," his mother said.

Alistair looked out to the horizon, and she sensed it to be true. She sensed that, somehow, things would never be the same on the Southern Isles again.

# CHAPTER EIGHTEEN

Thor rowed in the small boat, seated beside his companions, Reece, Elden, O'Connor, Conven, Indra and Matus, thrilled to be reunited with the familiar group, with his Legion brothers, and thrilled to also be joined by Matus. As the wind had died they had taken to the oars, and as they rowed, all of them settling into a gentle rhythm, the boat rocked gently on the calmly lapping waves. The rowing had been therapeutic for Thor, who found himself getting lost in the monotonous sound of the oar meeting water, leaning back and forward, feeling his muscles burn as he pulled on the oar.

Thor found himself getting lost in memories; he recalled his last battle, against Romulus and the dragons, and he found himself thinking of Mycoples and Ralibar, of all he had left behind. He felt as if he had lost so much, and he felt bad, as if he had let them down. Thor thought of the Ring, destroyed in his absence, and thought of how, if only he had stayed, perhaps he could have saved them all from the invasion, could have saved the Ring. Perhaps he could have saved Guwayne. He wished he could have done more, and sooner, and he wondered why fate had had to take the twists and turns that it had. Thor felt the guilt weighing heavily upon him.

Thor looked out at the horizon, as he had ever since they'd left, searching for any sign of Guwayne. He peered into the waters, but could see no sign of him; there had been too many false alarms, his mind tricking him again and again. Where could he be?

Thor blamed himself, of course. If he had only been here, perhaps none of this would have ever happened; yet then again, who knows if he would have been able to stop Romulus's entire nest of dragons. And if he had not gone to seek out his mother, perhaps he would have never had the power he needed to fight all those dragons and the Empire.

They rowed for hours, barely any wind at all, heading in a general northern direction, rolling up and down in the gentle ocean waves, fog rolling in and out, the sun coming in and out of the clouds. Finally, the others put down their oars and took a break, and Thor joined them, wiping sweat from the back of his brow.

"Where are we rowing, anyway?" O'Connor finally spoke up, breaking the silence, voicing the question that was on all of their minds. "To be honest with ourselves, we don't know where we are going."

A heavy silence fell over them, as no one was able to disagree; Thor, too, was having the same thoughts, but trying to suppress them. A part of him was an optimist, felt that Guwayne would appear if he rowed hard enough.

"We have to head in *some* direction," Reece countered. "And Gwen said the tide took him in north."

"That tide could have shifted at any time," Elden countered.

They all sat there, pondering.

"Well," Indra added, "the Queen had tried searching north herself, and she couldn't find him. As far as I know, there are no islands or any land this far north."

"Nobody really knows that," Matus said. "It is all uncharted."

Thor spoke up: "At least we are heading in one direction," he said. "At least we are searching. Whether we are going one way, or going another, we are covering ground."

"Yet our small boat in this vast sea could easily miss the boy," Indra said.

"Have you any better suggestions?" Matus asked.

They all fell silent. Of course, no one had any idea. Thor started to wonder if they all had faith, if they all felt, deep down, that finding Guwayne was a futile task, and if they had all just come to humor him.

"This might indeed be a futile task," Thor said, "but that does not mean it is not worth taking. Still, I am sorry to take you all from the ships."

Reece clasped a hand on his shoulder.

"Thorgrin, we would all go to the ends of the earth for you—and for your son. Without even any hope of finding him."

The others nodded, and Thor could see in their eyes that it was true. And he knew he would do the same for any of them.

Thor heard a sloshing noise, and he leaned over the edge of the boat and was surprised to see, swimming beside the boat, strange creatures he had never seen before. There were luminescent yellow creatures, like frogs, and they seemed to be jumping below the water. A school of them lit up the sea from underneath.

"I'm hungry," Elden said. "Perhaps we can catch one."

He leaned forward, but Matus grabbed his hand. Elden looked at him.

"They're poisonous," Matus said. "They congregate near the Upper Isles, too. Touch one, and you'll be dead in an instant."

Elden looked down at him with great respect and gratitude, and retracted his hand slowly, humbled.

Reece sighed as he stared out at the waters, and Thor studied him, concerned. Thor could see that his eyes were dull, joyless; he could tell that Reece, while he was away, had suffered, and was not the same youthful person he had known before he left. Thor recalled the story Gwen told him about Selese, and he felt compassion for Reece. Thor thought of the double wedding they'd almost had, back in the bountiful, flourishing Ring, and he realized how much had changed.

"You've been through much," Thor said to him.

"So have you," Reece replied.

"I'm sorry for your loss," Thor added. "Selese was a fine woman."

Reece nodded, grateful.

"You have lost someone, too," Reece said. "But we shall find him—if it is the last thing we do."

Conven, taking a break, came up and sat beside Thor and clasped his shoulder. Thor turned and saw Conven looking at him with respect.

"You saved me back in the Ring," Conven said, "in that prison. All the others had given up on me. I do not forget. I said I owe you, and I meant it. Now it is my turn to be by your side. I will find your son, or I shall die trying."

Thor clasped Conven's arm, and saw the hollow look in his face, a look of suffering, and he could see his mourning for his twin had still not left him. Thor realized that he, Reece, and Conven had all been to the edge of tragedy and back, all three of them shaped by suffering, all three not the same boys who had started in the Legion. They were all older now, more hardened. It seemed as if one by one, the Legion members were being tested, molded through suffering, each in their own way. Thor could only wonder what the future held for Elden, O'Connor, or Indra; he hoped it held nothing grim.

And then there was Matus, their new addition. Thor turned to him and nodded.

"I'm grateful to you for joining us," he said.

Matus came over and joined them.

"It is the least I can do," he replied. "I've always wanted to join the Legion, yet from my place on the Upper Isles I was never allowed to the mainland. I always wanted a chance to prove myself on the mainland, and embarking on a quest with you all is something I've always dreamed of."

"Now you should have it," Thor said. "Although it could be our quest sees few adversaries. I fear the sea and hunger might be the greatest foes before us."

Thor pondered their meager provisions, and he knew in but a few days they would run low. He knew they had to find land. He searched the horizon and tried not to think what would come of them if they did not.

Before he could finish the thought, suddenly, Thor felt a breeze on his face. At first it was a gentle wind. When it arrived, for some reason, he thought of his mother. He felt that she was with him, looking after him. The breeze grew stronger, and their lone canvas sail set to flapping, and Thor and the others looked up with gratitude.

They quickly hoisted it, and their boat began to move again.

"The wind is taking us east, not north," Reece observed. "Adjust the sails."

Thor felt a sudden buzzing on his wrist, and he looked down to see his bracelet glowing, the black diamond in its center sparkling. It suddenly grew warm, and he had a strong sensation that the wind was taking them in the right direction.

"Leave the sails as they are!" Thor commanded, as the others turned and looked at him with wonder. "The wind is taking us exactly where we need to go."

The boat began to gain speed, rocking in the waves, and Thor peered out to the horizon.

As they crested wave after wave, Thor finally saw something, a trace of something on the horizon. An outline. At first he thought it was another apparition; but then his heart skipped a beat as he realized it was real.

"Land!" O'Connor called out for all of them.

He confirmed what Thor already knew, what he had sensed from the breeze, from his bracelet. Land was before them. And Guwayne was in that direction.

*

Thor stood at the bow of the small boat, looking out with wonder as they approached the small island at full speed. The isle sat by itself in this vast sea, hardly a mile in diameter, ringed by bright white sands and gently lapping waves. Thor peered into its thick jungle, looking for any signs of his son.

It was a smooth landing as the tide carried them up right onto the sand, and Thor and the others disembarked as it did, grabbing the small boat and dragging it up firmly ashore.

Thor, excited, looked down at his bracelet; but it suddenly stopped glowing, and his heart fell as he sensed Guwayne was not on this place.

"I don't see any sign of Guwayne's boat landing here," O'Connor said. "We circled the whole island from sea, and there was nothing— no boat, no debris, no prints, nothing."

Thor shook his head as he said slowly, "My son is not here."

"How do you know?" Reece asked.

"I just know," Thor replied.

They all sighed with disappointment as they stood there, hands on hips, peering into the dense jungle before them.

"Well, we're here," Matus said. "Might as well look. Not to mention, we need food and water."

They all made their way onto the island, its white sands soon giving way to dense jungle. As they hiked, all was eerily quiet here except for the blowing of the wind off the sea, the rustling of the trees. As Thor paused to examine them, he saw they were all tall and thin, all bent over, with orange trunks, broad orange leaves, and large round fruits at the top, swaying in the wind.

"Waterfruits!" Elden called out in delight.

He grabbed one of the trees and shook it, harder and harder, making it sway, until finally one of them fell, landing in the sand beside him with a thump.

They all gathered around. It was as large as a watermelon, its skin green and fuzzy, and Elden stepped forward, removed his dagger, and stabbed it. He gouged a hole, gradually making it bigger, until it was large enough to drink from.

Elden lifted it to his mouth with both hands, and the clear water began to trickle out as he drank and drank.

He finally set it down and sighed with satisfaction; he handed it the others.

"The water's pure here, and sweet," he said. "It's delicious."

They passed it around and each of them drank, and soon it was finished. They all looked up to the other trees, thick with the fruits, the entire island swaying with them.

"We should stock up on them before we go," Thor said. "We can fill our boat."

"Don't forget the flesh," Matus said.

He stepped forward and knelt down and smashed the fruit open with the butt of his dagger, revealing soft white flesh inside. He reached down and used the tip of his dagger to pry it out, raised it to his lips, and took a bite. He chewed with satisfaction.

Thor grabbed a piece with the others, and as he chewed the chewy, sweet fruit, he felt rejuvenated.

They each turned and, without a word, spread out, each grabbing a tree and shaking it; one tree was stubborn, and Thor climbed to the top and knocked the fruit down with his fist.

They all set about gathering the fruit, and as they turned to walk together back to the boat, there came a sudden rustling behind them, and they all stopped in their tracks as one, looked at each other, and looked back. They peered into the thick foliage, wondering.

"Did you hear something?" Matus asked.

No one said a word, as they all stood there, frozen, watching.

The rustling came again.

A bush swayed, and Thor wondered what it could be; he hadn't heard any animal noises on the small island, or any traces of human life—and he didn't think this small island was big enough to support anything. Was it just the wind?

The rustling came again, and this time Thor's hairs turned on end. There was no mistaking it: something was out there.

As one, they all slowly dropped their fruits, turned, drew their swords, and faced the wall of foliage.

"I think something's watching us," Elden remarked.

"Then let's not make it wait," Conven said, and then he suddenly, without waiting, recklessly sprinted into the forest. Thor shook his head as he did, realizing that Conven was as suicidal as he had always been.

There came a shout, followed by Conven's cry, and they all chased after him, on his heels.

Thor and the others burst into a small clearing, and as he did, he stopped short, shocked by what he saw.

It was like something out of a nightmare. There was a gigantic spider, grotesquely large, five times taller than Thor, with eight hairy, thick legs, fifty feet long. Thor was horrified to see that one of them was wrapped around Conven, lifting him, examining him, and squeezing him as it opened its huge jaws and raised him toward it.

O'Connor stepped forward boldly and fired off three arrows at the spider's gigantic, purple eyes. One was a direct hit, and the creature shrieked and dropped Conven; he fell through the air and landed on the soft forest floor.

The spider, enraged, reached down and swiped O'Connor before he could react; O'Connor shrieked, a gash in his arm from the spider's razor-sharp claws. O'Connor sank to his knees, clutching his arm as it gushed blood, and as he did, the spider leaned down to eat him.

Elden rushed forward, raised his ax, and chopped the end of the spider's leg right before it could grasp Conven. The spider shrieked, gushing a green pus, and it swung around with one of its other legs and wrapped it around Elden. Elden cried out as it squeezed him, constraining his arms, and lifted him up to its mouth.

Thor rushed forward, the others beside him, and raised his sword high and reached up and stabbed the spider in the chest; it shrieked. Beside him, Indra threw her dagger, lodging it in the spider's eyes and Matus charged forward and sliced one of the spider's other legs. It dropped Elden and buckled, as if about to fall.

Yet as they watched, the spider, to Thor's shock, grew a brand new leg. It hissed, an awful sound, and as it opened its mouth wide, there suddenly emerged a massive silk web, shooting out and entangling them all. It was the stickiest thing Thor had ever felt, and as the spider wrapped it around them again and again, soon Thor found himself unable to move, completely restricted.

The spider hoisted them all up into the air, dangling before it, and examined them all, as if deciding which to eat first. It seemed to settle on Reece, and it leaned forward, opened its jaws, and prepared to eat him.

Thorgrin, helpless as the others, closed his eyes and summoned his inner power.

*Please, God. Do not abandon me. Not here, in this place. Do not allow my friends to die.*

Thor gradually felt a warmth rise up within him. He felt his inner power returning, recalling his time in the Land of the Druids; he began to feel the power of the spider, to feel the very fabric of the web, and inside him there grew an ancient and unmistakable power, stronger than any weapon, stronger than any man or any creature. He felt his mother's bracelet buzzing on his wrist, and he opened his eyes and looked.

A hole began burning right through the web, emanating from the diamond in his bracelet. It widened, and Thor felt his arm freed up. Soon, the hole burned even greater, and he felt himself freed from the web.

Thor turned and leapt for the spider's mouth, right before it could eat Reece, throwing himself inside it, planting his hands on its upper jaw and pushing higher and higher until the spider screeched and dropped Reece to the ground.

Thor spun out of the spider's jaw, and as he did, the spider snapped its mouth shut, barely missing killing him. In the same motion, Thor leapt upward and jumped onto the spider's back, raising his sword and plunging it in the back of its neck.

The spider's legs buckled, and it collapsed down to the ground, on its belly, shrieking.

One by one his Legion brothers disentangled themselves from the spider's web, and as they did, Thor used his power to move the web, to wrap the spider in it, again and again, until the spider was immobile, helpless, flailing in rage. Thor reached down and grabbed the web, spun it around with superhuman strength, then hurled it.

The spider went flying over the trees, through the air, until it finally landed far out into the ocean with a splash. It hissed and flailed, and they all watched as it slowly sank down into the sea.

The boys all exchanged a look of wonder, realizing how lucky they all were to be alive, how close they had come to death. As they all made their way back to the boats, Thor realized that, even in this empty sea, they could never again assume any place was safe.

# CHAPTER NINETEEN

Gwen, having handed off the baby to Illepra, knelt on the deck of the ship beside Argon, laying a gentle hand on his wrist. It was cold to the touch, as it had been ever since they had departed for this journey, and he still lay in the position in which she had left him. Gwen was heartbroken to see him like this, lying on his back, looking so frail, so weak, his eyes moving beneath his closed eyelids, as if he were living some dream, off in some other world.

"Argon, are you there?" she asked. "Come back to me."

He did not reply; he did not even flinch. Gwen felt that a part of Argon was still with her, but that another part was far away. She wondered if he would ever come back to her. He had given so much of himself to enable them all to survive, and Gwen felt guilty for it. She wanted now, more than ever, to be able to turn to him with questions, needing answers more than ever. Here she was, a Queen leading a nation in exile, heading to the most unlikely of places, right into the heart of the Empire. Gwen wondered if it was an insane plan, if they were all on their final death voyage as the currents pulled them further and further east, away from the Ring, away from the Upper Isles, and most of all, away from Guwayne and Thor.

Gwendolyn closed her eyes and felt a tear. She thought of Thor and Guwayne, out there in the sea somewhere, searching for each other, so far from her. It was a quest, she knew, from which they might not ever return. She wondered how fate could be so cruel to take Thorgrin away from her just at the moment she had seen him again. Were they ever destined to be together, in one place? Would they ever wed? Would they ever settle down together?

Gwen opened her eyes and saw that Argon would not be able to answer her now. She was on her own, and she would have to be strong, for all of her people.

Gwendolyn rose to her feet and walked to the side of the deck, looking out at the exotic creatures in this part of the sea, noticing all of her people standing at the edge of the railing, watching and wondering. She followed their gaze and looked up to the sky, and she blinked in surprise. Perhaps a hundred yards overhead, instead of clouds, there was an ocean, just like the ocean beneath him. At first she thought it was a reflection. But then she realized it was a real ocean, floating in the sky. Out of it fish leapt, upside down, then went back in.

It was the strangest thing she'd ever seen, and she could not fathom how it was possible.

Gwen scanned the horizon, and she saw rainbows—not just one, but hundreds of them. They were not shaped in arcs, but in circular cones, rising straight up from the ocean to the sky. There were cones of color everywhere, lighting up the sea.

Gwen heard a strange noise and looked up to see a huge bird, with a wing span perhaps twenty yards wide and a huge, grotesque head, circling above and shrieking. There appeared several more, swooping down, grabbing strange creatures out of the water, glowing, orange squid-like creatures, then swallowing them as they flew off.

The deeper into this sea they sailed, the more foreign everything became. The air smelled different here; the wind felt different. They were sailing deeper into a land Gwen had never known, a land she had never wished to know. She found herself missing home, missing the familiar, wanting to turn back, wanting everything just to be the way it was. But she forced herself to realize that the past was gone forever.

Gwen thought again of Guwayne, out there on the water, and her thoughts turned to Thorgrin. The farther away from them she sailed, the more she felt a heaviness in her chest, felt the likelihood increasing that she would never see them again. As she leaned over the rail, she extracted a quill and scroll of parchment from her waist, and she leaned against the wide, smooth rail and began to write:

*My dearest Thorgrin:*

*My love for you has not waned, nor shall it ever. I love you more than I can ever say, and I know you shall reunite us with our son. I want you to know the place you hold in my heart. I think of you and dream of you, and you are right here by my side. You are the only one I've ever loved, and I shall never stop loving you.*

*Your love forever,*

*Gwendolyn*

Gwendolyn took the scroll and rolled it up tight. She reached into her satchel and pulled out a small glass, took the cork off, put the letter inside, and sealed it back up. A tear rolling down her cheeks, she reached back and threw it. It went spinning through the air and landed with a soft splash in the sea.

As her unlikely message in a bottle floated on the waves, Gwendolyn half expected it to sink. She knew, of course, that there was no way that Thor would ever get it. And yet, she liked to think that somehow, by its entering the waters, he sensed it.

As Gwen watched the small bottle, she suddenly heard a screech high above, different from the other birds. She looked up, and her heart warmed to see her old friend, Estopheles, diving down low, zeroing in on the glass bottle. She dove down and rescued Gwen's message from the waters, swooping up the glass in her beak. She screeched as she flipped her great wings and carried it off, westward into the sky.

As Gwendolyn watched her go, her heart filled with wonder and hope.

*Estopheles,* she thought. *Find Thorgrin, and carry my message to him.*

Gwen heard a strange noise coming from a few feet away, on the other side of the deck. She looked over to see Sandara leaning over the rail, sprinkling flowers and ashes into the waters, and chanting in a strange language. Somehow, at the sight of her, Gwendolyn felt better. There was something about her, a healing quality, that made Gwendolyn feel at peace around her.

Sandara turned to look at her with her large black soulful eyes, and Gwendolyn quickly wiped away her tears, ashamed.

Sandara smiled and walked toward her, laying a hand on her shoulder. As she did, Gwendolyn felt a warmth seep into her, felt that somehow, despite everything, all would be okay.

\*

Sandara laid her hands on Queen Gwendolyn's shoulders, and she closed her eyes, chanting softly. She concentrated on sending her healing energy, and as she did, she could feel Gwendolyn's wounded spirit. She could feel all of the sadness within Gwendolyn, could feel her devastation at not being with her son, with her husband, Thorgrin. She could feel her uncertainty about the future, and she could also sense something else. She was not sure what. It felt like...regret about a decision she'd made. Something she had done in another world, a choice she'd had to make, having to do with sacrifice. She felt Gwen's tremendous guilt and uncertainty over the fate of her husband and her son.

Sandara felt tremendous heat leaving her palms and entering Gwendolyn as she focused on healing her. She opened her eyes, and as she did, she saw Gwendolyn wipe away her tears, and watched her expression lighten. She realized that her healing had worked; she had taken Gwen's sadness away. She shook her palms, which were burning her.

"I feel better around you," Gwen said. "Where did you learn your craft?"

Sandara smiled back.

"I am just another healer, my lady."

Gwendolyn shook her head and laid a hand on Sandara's shoulder.

"No," she replied. "You're far more than that. You have a gift."

Sandara smiled and looked away.

"My people," Sandara said, "they have different customs, different ways of healing. I come from a long line of healers. Seers, my people call them."

"Those flowers you dropped into the water earlier," Gwendolyn said. "What were they?"

"They were prayers for your husband and your son," Sandara said. "It is an ancient custom among my people. I prayed that the flowers would be carried on the tide, just as your boy and husband be carried on the tides back to you."

Sandara could see by Gwen's face how touched she was.

"I am looking forward to meeting your people," Gwendolyn said. "What are they like?"

Sandara sighed as she turned and looked out at the sea.

"My people are a very proud people. It is something of a paradox, as they have been slaves their entire lives. Yet they carry the pride of kings. They live with this paradox, each day."

"Sometimes the greatest pride lies within those who are subjugated," Gwen replied.

"Your words are true, my lady," Sandara said. "Just because one is a slave does not mean one is weak—it simply means they are outnumbered. But numbers change, and one day my people will rise up again."

"Will your people shelter us?" Gwen asked, concern in her voice.

Sandara sighed, wondering the same thing.

"My people take the laws of hospitality very seriously," she said. "And yet, the Empire is cruel, barbaric. If my people are caught harboring you, it will be death for them and their families."

A flash of concern crossed Gwendolyn's face.

"Perhaps we should go elsewhere in the Empire?"

Sandara shook her head.

"There is nowhere else," she said. "Not on this side of the empire. There are other places within the empire, other places of rebellion, but they will be longer and harder to get to—and in other places, the slaves are subjugated worse than us."

Gwendolyn looked at her meaningfully and nodded.

"Thank you," she said. "Whatever happens, thank you. You have helped us. You have given us a direction. Even if it does not work."

Sandara smiled, her eyes welling up; she felt so grateful toward Gwendolyn, who had taken her in from the start, and who had always been so kind to her.

"One day we might be sisters," Gwen added, with a smile.

Sandara blushed, recalling all of Kendrick's talk of marriage.

"I will do whatever I can, my lady," Sandara said, "to convince my people. You shall have my loyalty, whatever happens."

Several of Gwen's councilors approached and pulled her away, needing her attention on other matters, and Sandara soon found herself standing alone, looking out at the sea. She leaned over the railing, and wondered, trying to imagine the future that lay ahead of her. It would be so strange to be back home after all this time. How would her people receive her? Surely, they would be happy to see her; and yet, she would be arm in arm with Kendrick, a man of white skin. How would her people react? They could be very judgmental, she knew. More importantly, how would they react to her arriving with the ships? Would they turn them away?

As Sandara stood there, wondering, she felt a presence beside her, and she turned to see Kendrick coming up beside her, smiling down at her, draping an arm around her waist. She leaned in as he hugged her, and as always, she felt so comfortable in his arms.

"So we get to be together after all," he said.

Sandara smiled back.

"All that time in the Ring," he added, "you planned your return to the Empire, without me. And yet here we are, returning together. I suspect that if we hadn't all been exiled, you would have left without me."

Sandara nodded.

"Indeed I would have," she said. "Not because I do not love you, but because my people need me."

Kendrick nodded.

"Then at least," he said, "I shall be thankful for the one good thing the great war brought me."

Sandara studied his face, so noble, so beautiful, and she could see his love for her, and she felt a flash of concern.

"Kendrick, I love you deeply," she said. "I would like to think our love will withstand any obstacle, especially now that we shall be together in my homeland."

She fell silent, and he studied her, confusion written on his face.

"What do you mean?" he asked.

Sandara paused, wondering how to phrase it.

"My people," she explained, "they do not marry those of other races. Ours will be a first. Assuming, of course, you are even thinking of marriage."

Kendrick reached over and took her hand and looked her in the eyes.

"I've asked for your hand in marriage many times—and I would still like it now as much as ever."

Sandara smiled back up at him, feeling for the first time that maybe it was not a dream, that maybe it could really happen. And that scared her.

"What I am trying to say," she said, "is that I don't know how my people will react to you."

He looked at her carefully.

"I did not take you to be one who bows to the will of her people," he said.

Sandara reddened, indignant.

"I am my own person," she replied. "I bow to no one. And yet, my people are very close to one another. The disapproval of the elders is not something easily tolerated. I do not wish to be an outcast among my family."

Kendrick's face darkened as he turned and looked out to the sea.

"I would be, for you," he said.

"Your people are more open-minded than mine," she countered. "You do not know what it's like. The people of the Ring, they marry those of other races, from all parts of the world."

"And yet if they did not," Kendrick said, "I would not let their disapproval stop me from being with someone I love."

Sandara turned to him, frustrated.

"You cannot say that," she said, "because you do not know what it's like."

He sighed.

"The choice is yours, my lady," he said. "I will not ask you to be with someone you do not wish to be with."

Sandara felt her heart breaking inside. She reached out for his hands, raised them to her lips, and kissed them.

"Kendrick, you do not understand me. What I am trying to say is that I want to be with you. I don't want my people to tear us apart. But I will need to be strong. I will need your strength."

He nodded, and looked at her intently.

"I would walk through fire to be with you," he said. "The disapproval of your people will not drive me away."

Sandara felt relieved, as if she'd let a great weight off her chest, and she leaned it to kiss him; but suddenly, she noticed something out of the corner of her eye, something that made her stop. She looked carefully, studying the ocean waters, and her heart dropped as she was flooded with panic. She saw that, beneath them, the waters of the sea were shifting colors, growing lighter and lighter.

Kendrick followed her gaze.

"What is it?" he asked, seeing her expression.

"Turn around!" she yelled, grabbing his shoulders. "Do not look at the water!"

126

Sandara didn't take time to respond to Kendrick's puzzled look, but instead turned and suddenly yelled out to one of the Queen's attendants: "Sound the bells! Warn the people! Do not look down! No matter what! GO!" She shoved the sailor, and he stumbled off, yelling the warning throughout the ship, and climbing the mast to sound the bells.

Soon the bells started to toll, and shouts sounded all throughout the ships as they burst into chaos.

"What has gotten into you!?" Kendrick asked.

But Sandara was busy studying the others; she looked around and saw many people rushing to the railings, on all the ships, leaning over and looking down at the light waters. Desperate to save them, she ran to the ship's side, grabbed people from behind, and yanked them back before they could look over.

Kendrick saw what she was doing, and he joined in, and together, they managed to save quite a few of them.

But they could not reach them all, and for the others, for those who did not listen, it was too late. Sandara watched with horror as one person after another, staring down at the waters, turned to stone.

They fell over the rail, one after the next, the air filled with the sounds of stones splashing into the water, as they plummeted one after another into the sea of death.

# CHAPTER TWENTY

Volusia sat on her marble throne, impatient, impetuous, staring back at the two common prisoners who stood shackled before her. Beyond them, in the distance, down below, there rose the chants of a hundred thousand of her citizens, squeezed into the coliseum, all cheering as the Razif was let loose in the arena. Volusia, not wanting to be distracted from the big moment, looked past these riffraff and down over their shoulders and saw the beast, bright red, nearly the size of an elephant, with three horns and a wide square face and jaw, and a hide as thick as a hundred swords, charging madly through the arena. The ground trembled as it charged in circles on the dirt floor, again and again, in a rage, looking for any victim.

The crowd cheered wildly at the expectation of the blood sport that would follow.

Volusia's cold black eyes turned and settled on the two men standing before her. She studied them with disinterest, and as she did, she watched the expression of these middle-aged men softening at the sight of her, saw a new hope in their eyes, and something else: lust. Volusia had always had this effect on men. Although she had barely reached her seventeenth year, Volusia had already lived long enough to witness the effect she had—every man and woman she'd ever met acknowledged that she was gorgeous, and she did not need them to tell her; when she glanced into a mirror, which was often, she saw it herself. With her black eyes and raven black hair falling down to her waist, her perfectly chiseled features, her skin white as alabaster, she was not like others of her race.

Volusia was different from them in every way, she, of the human race who had nonetheless managed to ascend to leader of the Empire race of this Empire city, like her mother before her. This city might not be the capital of the Empire, but it was, at least the capital of the Northern Region of the Empire, and if it were not for Romulus, no one would stand in her way. Indeed, Volusia considered herself, not Romulus, to be the undisputed leader of the Empire, and very soon she planned to prove it. There had always been a rivalry between the

South and the North, an uneasy alliance, and up until recently, Volusia had been content to allow Romulus to think he held all the power. It was advantageous for her to be thought of as weak.

Of course, she was the farthest thing from it, as anyone in her city knew too well.

As Volusia stared at the two men gaping at her, she shook her head at how stupid they were, looking upon her as a sex object. Clearly, they did not know of her reputation. Volusia had not risen to become Empress of the entire Northern Empire through her good looks; she had risen because of her ruthlessness. She was, indeed, more ruthless than all the men, more ruthless than all the generals, more ruthless than all the great nobles that had served in the House of Lords for centuries—more ruthless, even, than her own mother, whom she had strangled with her own bare hands.

Volusia tracked her ruthlessness back to the day when her mother had sold her to that brothel. Just twelve years old when her mother, who had more riches than she could count, had decided that she was going to sell Volusia off into a life of hell—just for the fun of it—Volusia had been shocked when she had been escorted into a small, stale room and given her first customer. But her customer—a fat, greasy man in his fifties—had been even more shocked when he'd encountered, instead of an accommodating girl, a remorseless killer. Volusia had surprised even herself when she'd made her first kill, surprising him by wrapping a cord around his neck and strangling him with all her might. He had fought relentlessly, but she had not let go.

What had surprised Volusia most was not her courage, or her ruthlessness, or her lack of hesitation—but how much she had enjoyed killing him. She had learned at an early age that she had a talent for killing, and a great joy for it; she just loved inflicting pain on others, a far greater pain than they intended to inflict on her.

Volusia murdered her way out of the brothel, and had kept on murdering, killing her way all the way up into the house of power of Volusia, finally taking her own mother's life, and taking the throne. She had slept with men too, when it suited her—but she always killed them when she was through with them. She didn't like to leave a trail of anyone who had come into contact with her; she considered herself a goddess, and above having to interact with anyone.

Now, at only seventeen, Volusia, having consolidated power in her great city, sat on her mother's throne, having amassed so much power that the entire city cowered before her. Volusia knew that she was special. Other rulers of other Empire provinces wielded brutality for the purposes of power; Volusia, though, thoroughly enjoyed it. She was willing to go farther, to be more extreme, to do more than anyone else who might get in her way. She thought it more than ironic that she was named after her city, as if she were always destined to rule. She thought it was destiny.

"My Empress," a royal guard announced cautiously, "these two captives brought before you have been caught slandering your name in the streets of Volusia."

Volusia look them up and down. They were stupid men, peasants, shackled, dressed in rags, looking at her with their lowly grins. One of them stared back at her during the pronouncement, while the other looked nervous and contrite.

"And what have you to say for yourself?" she asked, her voice dark, deep, nearly like the voice of a man.

"My lady, I've said no such thing," said the captive who was trembling. "I was misheard."

"And you?" she asked, turning to the other.

He stuck up his chin and looked at her defiantly.

"I slandered your name," he admitted, "and you deserve slandering. You are a young girl still, and yet have built a sadistic reputation. You don't deserve to sit on the throne."

He looked her up and down as if she were a mere sex object, and Volusia stood up, sticking out her chest, which was considerable, standing erect with her perfect figure. Her eyes lit up as a he continued to stare at her; these men sickened her. *All* men sickened her.

Volusia stepped forward slowly toward them, looking them over, and finally approached the one who was leering at her. She got close to him, removed a small metal hook, and in one quick motion, she thrust it upward, beneath his chin, through his mouth, hooking him like a fish.

He shrieked and dropped to his knees as blood burst from his throat. Volusia pulled the hook harder and harder, enjoying his squirming, until finally, he collapsed to the ground, dead.

Volusia turned to the other, who was now positively shaking, and approached him, enjoying her morning immensely.

The captive dropped to his knees, quivering.

"Please, my lady," he pleaded. "Please, don't kill me."

"Do you know why I killed him?" she asked.

"No my lady," he said, weeping.

"Because he told the truth," she said derisively. "I granted him a merciful death because he was honest. But you are less than honest. You shall get a less than merciful death."

"No, my lady! NO!" he shrieked.

"Stand him up," Volusia ordered her men.

Her guards rushed forward, grabbed the man, lifted him up as he quivered, and stood him before her.

"Back him up," she commanded.

They did as she commanded, backing him to the edge of the marble terrace. There was no railing, nothing between the edge and the drop down to the arena below, and the man looked over his shoulder, terrified.

Down below stormed the Razif, to the taunting of the crowd, waiting for the contestants to arrive.

"I do not find you worthy to live," Volusia pronounced. "But I do find you worthy of being my entertainment."

Volusia took two steps forward, lifted her foot, and shoved him in the chest, knocking him backwards off the balcony with her silver boots.

He shrieked as he tumbled through the air, falling downwards, bouncing off of the sloped walls, then finally tumbling and landing down into the dirt arena.

The crowd cheered wildly, and Volusia stepped forward and looked down, watching as the Razif set its sights on the man. The man, bloody but still alive, stumbled to his feet and tried to run; but the beast's rage was great as it charged, the crowd's cheering goading him on, and in moments, it gorged the captive with three horns to the back.

The crowd was ecstatic as the Razif held him up high above his head, victoriously, and paraded his trophy in a broad lap around the arena.

The crowd went crazy, and as Volusia stood there and watched, taking it all in, she thrived on the man's pain. It brought her a joy she could not describe.

Down below, horns sounded, gates were opened, and dozens of shackled slaves were dumped into the arena. The crowd roared as the Razif tracked each slave down and tore them all to pieces, one at a time.

A distant horn sounded, from the ports, and Volusia looked to the horizon, already bored by what was going on below her. She watched people get torn to pieces every day, and she was craving a more interesting form of torture. The horn she'd just heard was unique, announcing the arrival of a dignitary, and Volusia looked to the horizon and saw in the distance, out at sea, three Empire ships sailing toward her, bearing the distinct banner of the Romulus's army.

"It seems the great Romulus has returned," one of her advisors said, coming to stand beside her, looking out.

"When he left, his fleet filled the horizon," said another advisor. "Yet he now returns with a mere three ships. Why does he come here, to us? Why not to the South?"

Volusia watched carefully, hands on her hips, and she studied them, taking it all in. She had a great skill to grasp a situation far before any of the others, and she did once again, knowing immediately what was happening here.

"There is only one thing that would drive Romulus to return here, to us, to this part of the Empire, before going on. It is shame," she said. "He comes here because his fleet has been destroyed. He cannot return to the capital without a fleet—it would be a sign of weakness. He's come to us to replenish his ships first, before sailing to the heart of the Empire."

Volusia smiled wide.

"He presumes that my part of the Empire is weaker than his. And that will be his downfall."

As Volusia watched his ships approach, she knew that soon he would be in her harbor, and she felt her blood rush in excitement. It was the moment of her life she had been waiting for: her enemy was being brought right into her hands. He had no idea. He had underestimated her; they all had.

Volusia couldn't stop smiling; the fates indeed smiled down on her. She always knew she was meant to be the greatest of them all—and now the fates had proven it true. Soon, she would kill him. Soon, it would all be hers.

# CHAPTER TWENTY-ONE

Darius felt every muscle in his body burning as he swung ten feet off the ground, hanging by his hands from a bamboo pole. Every muscle in his body cried for him to just let go, to hit the ground, to give in to the sweet release—but he would not allow himself to. He was determined to pass the test.

Groaning, Darius looked around and saw dozens of his brothers in arms already collapsed on the mud, having dropped from their poles, unable to take the pain of hanging. He was determined to outlast them. It was one of the rites of their training, to see which boy could last the longest before dropping, one of the ways to gain respect of the others. Only four other boys remained hanging, and he was determined to outwait them; as the youngest and smallest of the lot, he needed to prove his toughness.

Filling Darius's ears were the cheers of the others, encouraging them to hang or to fall. Another boy beside him slipped, and Darius heard him hit the mud. There came another cheer.

Now there were three of them. Darius's palms burned as he hung from the bamboo, the branch sagging, his shoulders feeling as if they would come loose from their sockets. Down below he saw the disapproving eyes of his instructors, watching over him, and Darius was intent on proving them wrong. He knew that they expected him to fail—and he knew what he did not have in size and age he could make up for in spirit.

Another boy dropped, there came another cheer, and now there were just Darius and one other boy left hanging. Darius glanced over and saw who it was—Desmond—a boy twice as large and tall as he, one of the most respected of all the boys. They were slaves by day, but they considered themselves warriors by night, and as they trained together at night, they had a hierarchy, a fierce code of honor and respect. If they could not get respect from the Empire, they could get it from themselves, and these boys lived and died for this respect. If they could not fight against the Empire, at least they could train and compete amongst themselves.

As Darius's limbs ached with an unspeakable pain, he closed his eyes and willed himself to hang on. He wondered how much pain Desmond could endure, how much longer it would take him to drop. This contest meant more to Darius than he could say, and a reflex was prompting him to use his hidden powers.

But Darius shook the thought from his mind, forcing himself not to use magic, not to have any unfair advantage; he wanted to beat the others with force of will alone.

His sweaty palms slipping from the bamboo, one inch at a time, he was beginning to slide. He was seeing stars as his ears were filled with the shouts and cries of the boys below, sounding a hundred miles away. He wanted more than anything to hold on, but as he slipped, soon he was hanging on by just his fingertips.

Darius grunted as he closed his eyes and felt himself about to pass out. He knew in another second he would have to release.

Just before he let go, Darius heard a sudden slip, heard a body fall through the air and land in the mud, and heard a loud cheer. He opened his eyes to see Desmond on the ground, collapsed in exhaustion. The boys cheered, and Darius somehow summoned the strength to hang on for a few more seconds, basking in his victory. He did not just want to win; he wanted a clear and firm victory, wanted the others to see and to know that he was the strongest.

Finally, he let himself go, his shoulders giving on him as he fell through the air and landed in the mud.

Darius rolled to his side, his shoulders on fire, and before he could nurse his exhaustion, he felt a dozen boys jumping on him in congratulations, cheering, yanking him to his feet. Covered in mud, Darius struggled to catch his breath as the crowd parted ways and his commander, Zirk, a true warrior, wide as a tree trunk, with no shirt and rippling muscles, stepped forward.

The crowd quieted as Zirk looked down on him, expressionless.

"Next time you win," Zirk said, his voice deep, "hold on longer. It is not enough to win: you must crush your opponents."

Zirk turned and walked away, and Darius watched him go, disappointed he had not received any praise. Then again, he knew that was the way of the instructors. Any attention, any words from them, should be considered approval.

"Choose a partner!" Zirk boomed, facing the others. "It is time for wrestling!"

"But our shoulders have not even recovered yet!" protested one of the boys.

Zirk turned to him.

"That is exactly why we must wrestle now. Do you think your opponent in battle will give you time to recover? You must learn to fight at your weakest, and learn at that moment to fight your best."

The boys began to break off into positions, and as they did, Desmond came up beside Darius.

"Nice job back there," Desmond said, extending a hand.

They clasped forearms, and Darius was surprised. It was the first time Desmond had paid him any attention.

"I underestimated you," Desmond said. "You're not as weak as you look." He smiled.

Darius smiled back.

"Is that a compliment?"

They were separated in the chaos, as boys got between them, hurrying every which way to pair up with each other for wrestling. Beside him, the one boy in the group that Darius did not like—Kaz, a bulky boy with a square jaw and narrow, mean eyes—ran over to Luzi, the smallest boy of the group, and grabbed him by the shirt. Luzi had initially paired off with someone close to his size, but Kaz yanked him away and made him face him.

"You will wrestle with me," Kaz said.

Luzi looked up at him, terrified.

"It won't be a match," Luzi said. "You are three times my size."

Kaz smiled casually back, a cruel look to his face.

"I can wrestle with anyone I choose to," he said. "Maybe you will learn something. Or maybe, after your beating, you will leave our group."

Darius felt the heat rise to his cheeks as he felt the indignity of it. Darius could not stand to see injustice anywhere, and he could not allow himself to sit idly by.

Without thinking, Darius suddenly stepped between them, facing Kaz. He looked up at Kaz, taller than him by a head and twice as wide, and he forced himself not to look away, and not to feel fear.

"Why don't you wrestle with *me*?" Darius said to him.

Kaz's expression darkened as he stared back at Darius.

"You can hang from a branch, boy," he said, "but that doesn't mean you can fight. Now get out of my way, or I'll pummel you, too."

Kaz reached out to shove him away, but Darius did not move; instead, he stood there, resolute, and smiled back.

"Then pummel me," he said. "You might—but I will fight back. I might lose, but I will not back down."

Kaz, furious, reached out to grab Darius and throw him out of his way. But as soon as Kaz's hand reached his shirt, Darius used a trick he'd learned from one of the teachers: he waited until the last moment, then grabbed Kaz's wrist in a lock and spun it around, twisting his arm behind his back. Darius threw him face down to the mud, sending him sliding across the clearing, then jumped on top of him, beginning the wrestling match.

All the boys in the forest clearing took notice, and they all crowded around them, cheering, as Darius felt himself spinning, being thrown by Kaz's great bulk as he wheeled around. Darius slid across the mud, and before he could react, Kaz was on top of him. Kaz's weight and strength were too much for him, and soon Kaz pinned him down.

"You little rat," Kaz seethed. "You're going to pay for this."

Kaz spun around, and Darius felt his arm being yanked behind his back; the pain was excruciating, and it felt as if it were about to be broken off.

Darius felt his face buried in the mud, as Kaz leaned in close behind him, his hot breath on the back of his neck. The pain in his arm was indescribable as Kaz yanked it back even further.

"I can break your arm right now if I choose to," Kaz hissed in his ear.

"Then do it," Darius groaned back. "It still won't change who you are: a coward."

Kaz pulled his arm back harder, and Darius groaned, feeling that Kaz was about to break it.

Suddenly, Darius heard footsteps running across the mud, and he saw, from the corner of his eye, Luzi appear and jump on Kaz's back.

Kaz, enraged, let go of Darius's arm, stood up, and threw Luzi, who went flying through the air.

Darius spun around, nursing his aching arm, to see Kaz turn back around for him. Darius braced himself for another blow—when suddenly Desmond arrived, blocking Kaz's way.

"Enough," Desmond said to Kaz, his voice filled with authority. "You've had your fun."

Kaz stared Desmond back, and Darius could see the hesitation, then uncertainty in his eyes. Clearly, he was afraid of Desmond.

"I'm not done," Kaz said.

"I said you are," Desmond repeated, expressionless, unmoving.

Kaz stared him down for several seconds, then finally, he must have realized it wasn't worth it; slowly, he backed away.

The tension dissipated, the boys going back to their lines, Darius looked up and saw Desmond reach down a hand for him. He took it and was pulled back up to his feet.

"That was brave of you," Desmond said. "Stupid. But brave."

Darius smiled.

"Thanks," he said. "You spared me a lot worse."

Desmond shook his head.

"I admire bravery," he said. "However foolish."

Suddenly, a distinct sound cut through the clearing; it was the sound of a horn, a low, somber horn, vibrating through the trees.

The boys all froze and looked at each other, their faces grave. That horn only meant one thing: it was the horn of death. It could only mean that one of their own had been killed.

"Everyone to the village at once!" commanded Zirk, and Darius fell in with the others, Desmond, Luzi, and Raj falling in by his side, as they made their way for the village. Darius braced himself, knowing it could not be good.

*

Darius hurried with his brothers in arms straight into the chaotic center of their small village, people filtering into the packed center as the horn of death blew again and again. Darius walked on the narrow dirt road, filled with chickens and dogs running about, and he passed small brown homes built of clay and mud, with thatched roofs that let in too much rain. The homes in this village were too close to each other, and Darius often wondered why he and his people could not live someplace else.

The soft, low horn blew again, the sound rising up, reverberating throughout the hills, and more and more villagers streamed in. Darius had not seen so many of his people in one place in as long as he could remember, and he felt people bumping him on all sides, shoulder to shoulder, as he reached the village center.

The crowd fell silent as the village elders appeared, taking their seats around the stone well in the center of town. Salmak, the leader of the elders, stood solemnly, and as he did, all were silent. He faced them all, with his long white beard and fraying robes, and raised a single palm high in the air, and the horn stopped. The tension in the silence hung over them all like a blanket.

"The collapse on the mountainside," he said slowly, his voice grave, "brought the death of twenty-four of our brethren."

Moans and cries arose from the crowd, and Darius felt his stomach drop. As always, he braced himself for the list of names, hoping and praying that none of his cousins or aunts or uncles were on it.

"Gialot, son of Oltevo," Salmak called out in his somber voice, and as he did, a mother's cry ripped through the air. Darius turned and saw a woman weeping, tearing her clothes, dropping to her knees and putting dirt on her head.

"Onaso, son of Palza," the chief continued.

Darius closed his eyes and shook his head as all around him came the sound of wailing and crying, as name after name filled the air. Each name felt like a nail in his coffin, like a hole in his heart; Darius felt like it would never end. He knew most of the names, some distant acquaintances.

"Omaso, son of Liutre."

Darius froze: that was a name he really knew, the name of one of his brothers in arms. At the announcement, his brothers all gasped. Darius closed his eyes and imagined his friend's death, imagined him being crushed by all that rock and dirt, and he felt sick. He also knew that it could easily have been him instead; just last week, Darius had been assigned to work those cliffs.

Finally, the names stopped, and there came a long silence. The crowd began to slowly disperse, the air somber, and Darius and the other boys stood there, staring at each other. They all looked indignant, as if knowing that something needed to be done.

Yet Darius knew that they would do nothing. It was the way of his people, the way it had always been. His people would all die, either directly by the taskmasters, or indirectly through labor, and it had become their lot, their way of life. No one ever seemed willing to change it.

This time, though, the deaths affected Darius more than usual; it seemed there were more names, more grief. Darius wondered if it was worse, or if he was just growing older, becoming less able to tolerate the status quo he had always lived with.

Without thinking, Darius stepped forward into the village center, without even asking permission from the elders. Before he could even think of what he was doing, he found himself yelling out, his voice piercing the air:

"And how long shall we suffer these indignities?" he cried out.

The crowd froze, and all eyes turned to him as there came a heavy silence.

"We are dying here, each day. When will enough be enough?"

There came a murmur from the crowd, and Darius felt a hand on the back of the shoulder. He turned to see his grandfather looking down sternly at him, trying to yank him away.

Darius knew he was in trouble; he knew it was a sign of great insolence to show anything but respect toward the elders, and to speak without permission. But on this day, Darius didn't care; on this day, he'd had enough.

He brushed off his grandfather's hand and stood his ground, facing the elders.

"They outnumber us more than the sands of the sea," an elder said back. "If we rise up, by day's end we would be gone. Better to be alive than to be dead."

"Is it?" Darius called out. "I say it's better to be dead than to live as dead men."

A long murmur came from the crowd, none of his villagers used to hearing any defiance of the elders. His grandfather yanked on his shirt again, but Darius would not move.

Salmak stepped forward and glared down at him.

"You speak without permission," he said slowly, gravely. "We will forgive your words as those of a hasty youth. But if you continue to incite our people, if you continue to show disrespect to your elders, you will be lashed in the town square. We shall not warn you again."

"This meeting is finished!" another elder yelled out.

The crowd began to slowly disperse all around Darius, and his cheeks burned with the indignity of it all. He loved his people, but he disrespected them at the same time. They all seemed so complacent to him, and he did not feel he was cut from the same cloth as they. He was terrified of becoming like them, of growing old enough here to think as they did, to see the world as they did. Darius felt he was still young enough and strong enough to have independent thought. He knew he needed to act on that while he still could, before he became old and complacent. Before he became like the town elders, trying to silence anyone who held a dissenting view, anyone with passion.

"You are really looking to get a beating, aren't you?" came a voice.

Darius turned to see Raj come up beside him with a smile, clasping him on the shoulder.

"I didn't think you had it in you," Raj added. "I'm getting to like you more and more. I think you might just be as crazy as I."

Before Darius could respond, he turned to find one of his commanders, Zirk, standing over him, a disapproving look across his face.

"It is not your place to propose action," he said. "It is ours. A true warrior knows not only how to fight, but when to. That is something you have yet to learn."

Darius faced him, determined, not willing to back down this time.

"And when is the time to fight?" he asked.

Zirk's eyes burned back with fury, clearly unhappy at being questioned.

"The time is when we say it is."

Darius grimaced.

"I've lived in this village my entire life," Darius said, "and that time has never come. And I sense it never will. You are all so intent on protecting what we have, that you won't see that we have nothing."

Zirk shook his head disapprovingly.

"These are the words of a youth," he said. "You would rush into battle, into a sure death, just to relieve your passion. You, who are so small that you cannot even beat your brethren in battle. What makes you think you can beat the Empire? You, with no weapons, unarmed?"

"We have weapons," Darius countered.

Desmond came up beside them, along with several of his brothers. They all crowded around, and as they did, Kaz stepped forward and laughed derisively.

"We have bows and slings and weapons made of bamboo," he said. "Those are not weapons. We have no steel. And you expect to battle against the finest armor and weaponry and horses of the Empire? You will incite others and get them all killed. You should stay in our village and keep your mouth shut."

"Then what do we train for?" Darius challenged. "For wrestling matches in the forest? For an enemy we are too afraid to face?"

Zirk stepped forward and pointed a finger in Darius's face.

"If you're unhappy, you can leave us," he said. "Joining our force is a privilege."

Zirk turned his back on him and walked away, and the other boys, too, began to leave.

Raj looked at him and shook his head in admiration.

"Upsetting everyone today, aren't you?" Raj asked with a smile.

"I am with you," came a voice.

Darius turned to see Desmond standing there. "I'd rather die on my feet than live on my back."

Before Darius could reply, he felt a hand on his shoulder, and he turned to see a small man wearing a cloak and hood, and gesturing for him to follow. Darius looked all around, then back at the man, wondering who he was.

The man turned and walked away quickly, and Darius, intrigued, followed after him through the crowd, weaving his way in every direction.

The man weaved his way in and out, between houses, to the far side of the village before he finally stopped before a small clay home. He pushed back his hood as he faced him, and Darius saw his large, darting eyes that looked about cautiously.

"If your words are not empty words," the man said in a whisper, "I have steel. I have weapons. Real weapons."

Darius stared at him, eyes widening in awe. He had never met anyone who had possessed steel before, as owning it was on pain of death, and he wondered where he'd gotten it.

"When you are ready, find me," the man added. "The last clay house by the river. Speak to no one of this. If anyone asks, I will deny it."

The man turned and hurried off into the crowd, and Darius watched him, wondering, his mind swarming with questions. Before he could call out after him, Darius felt yet another strong hand on his shoulder, spinning him around.

Darius saw the face of his disapproving grandfather, his face lined with age, framed by his short, gray hair, scowling down at him. He was, though, surprisingly strong and vibrant for his age.

"That man leads to death," his grandfather warned sternly. "Not just for you, but for all of your kin. Do you understand me? We have survived for generations, unlike other slaves in other provinces, because we have never embraced steel. If the Empire catches you with it, they will raze our village to the ground, and will kill every single one of us," he said, jabbing his finger in his chest to drive home his point. "If I catch you seeking out that man, you will be banished from our family. You will not be welcome in our home. I shall not say this again."

"Papa—" Darius began.

But his grandfather had already turned and stormed back into the village.

Darius watched him go, upset. He loved his grandfather, who had practically raised him since the disappearance of his own father years ago. Darius respected him, too. But he did not share his view on complacency. He never would. His grandfather was of another generation. And he would never understand. *Never.*

Darius turned back to the crowd, and one face caught his attention. Standing there, about twenty feet away, was the girl, the one he had seen in the Alluvian Forest. People passed by in front of her, yet she kept her eyes fixed upon Darius, as if no one else in the world existed.

Darius's heart pounded at the sight of her, and the rest of the world melted away. This girl had captivated his thoughts since he had laid eyes upon her, and seeing her now, here, felt surreal. He had wondered if he would ever see her again.

Darius pushed his way through the crowd, heading toward her. He was afraid she might turn away, but she stood there, proudly, staring back, and it was unmistakable that she was looking at him. Her face was expressionless. She did not smile—but she did not frown either.

Darius looked into her soulful yellow eyes, and below them he could see the small welt on her cheek where the taskmaster had struck her. He felt a fresh wave of indignity, and more than anything, he felt a connection with her, something stronger than he'd ever felt.

He broke through the crowd and stood a few feet away from her. He did not know what to say, and they both stood there, facing each other, in the silence.

"I heard your words, in the village," she said. Her voice was deep and strong, the most beautiful voice he'd ever heard. "Are they hollow?" she asked.

Darius flushed.

"They are not hollow," he replied.

"So what action do you plan on taking?" she asked.

He stood there, not sure how to respond. He had never met anyone as direct as her.

"I...don't know," he said.

She studied him.

"I have four brothers," she said. "They are warriors. They think the same way as you. And I have already lost one of my brothers because of it."

Darius looked at her, surprised.

"How?" he asked.

"He went off by himself, one night, to wage war with the Empire. He killed a few taskmasters. But they caught him, and they killed him horribly. Cruelly. He had stripped himself of all his markings, so they couldn't track him back to us, or they would have killed us all, too."

She looked at Darius as if debating something.

"I don't want to be with a man who is like my brother," she finally said. "There is room for pride among boys—but not among men. Because men must back up pride with action. And action for us means death."

Darius looked at her, taken aback by her words, her eyes so strong, so powerful, never wavering from his. He was in awe of her. She spoke with the strength and wisdom of a queen, and he could hardly understand how he was looking back at a girl his own age.

More than anything, as he stood there, his heart pounding, he wondered why she was talking to him. He wondered if she liked him, if she had the same feelings for him that he had for her. Did she like him? Or was she just trying to help him?

"So tell me, then," she finally said, after a long silence. "Are you a you a man? Or a hero?"

Darius did not know how to respond.

"I am neither," he said. "I am just myself."

She stared at him long and hard, as if summing him up, as if trying to decide.

Finally, she turned and began to walk away. Darius's heart was falling, as he assumed he'd given her the wrong answer, that she changed her mind.

But as she walked away, she turned her head to him, and for the first time, and said:

"Meet me at the river, beneath the weeping tree, as the sun sets," she said. "And don't keep me waiting."

She disappeared into the crowd, and Darius's heart pounded as he watched her go. He had never encountered anyone like her, and he had a feeling that he never would. For the first time ever, a girl had taken a liking to him.

Or had she?

# CHAPTER TWENTY-TWO

Alistair stood on the stone plaza in the breaking light of dawn, high up on the cliffs, joined by Erec's mother and all her advisors, and looked out over the sweeping vistas of the Southern Isles. Down below, she could see the battle raging, as it had been all night since her encounter with Bowyer. Alistair looked out at this beautiful isle, draped by a morning mist, wafting with the smell of lemon blossoms, now erupted in war—and she felt guilty that she had been the one to spark this civil war.

Yet at the same time she felt vindicated, relieved that these people finally realized she was innocent—and that Bowyer was the assassin. She knew that Bowyer needed to be stopped before he stole the kingship—after all, the kingship belonged to Erec—and Alistair was determined to see that Erec recovered, and claimed what was rightfully his. Not because she wanted to be Queen—she did not care for title or rank—but because she wanted her husband-to-be to receive what he deserved.

Erec's mother, beside her, watched the battles with concern, and Alistair reached over and laid a hand on her wrist. Alistair felt overwhelmed with gratitude towards her, for standing by her side the entire time.

"I owe you a great deal of thanks," Alistair said. "If it were not for you, I would be sitting in that dungeon—or dead—right now."

Erec's mother smiled back, although her smile was weak, as she looked back at the battle below, grave with concern.

"And I owe you as much," she said. "You saved my son's life."

She studied the cliffs below and her brow furrowed.

"And yet, if this battle does not go well, I fear it may all be for nothing," she added.

Alistair looked at her in surprise.

"Are you concerned?" she asked. "I thought Bowyer rules but one of the twelve provinces. What danger could there be when there are eleven united against one?"

Alistair's mother watched the battle, expressionless.

146

"My former husband was always wary of the Alzacs," she said. "They do not only produce the best warriors on the island, but they are also crafty, and not to be trusted. They are also power hungry. I will not rest easy until I see every one of them involved in the rebellion slaughtered."

Alistair watched the battle, and saw thousands of Southern Islanders pushing back Bowyer's tribe, the battle raging up and down steep mountain slopes, spread out all over the Southern Isles, men fighting men on steep angles, the distant sound of metal clashing against metal and horses neighing punctuation the morning air. They were all brilliant warriors, their copper armor and weaponry shining in the sun, and they blanketed the mountains like goats, fighting each other to the death.

She watched and flinched as one soldier off his horse and off the side of the cliff, shrieking as he went hurtling to his death.

As far as Alistair could tell, the Southern Islanders had the advantage over Bowyer's tribe, which appeared to be on the run, and she could not see what there was to fear. Perhaps the former Queen was being overly cautious. Soon, she felt, this would all be over, Erec would be back in his seat as King, and they could start over again.

Alistair heard a shuffling of feet, and she turned and saw Dauphine walking toward her from the far side of the plaza. Dauphine had, in the past, always approached her with a look of disapproval or indifference—yet this time, Alistair noticed she wore a different expression. It seemed to be one of remorse—and of a new respect.

Dauphine came up to her.

"I must apologize," she said earnestly. "You stood falsely accused. I was misinformed, and for that I am sorry."

Alistair nodded back.

"I never held any ill feelings toward you," Alistair said, "and I do not harbor them now. I am happy to have you as my sister-in-law, assuming you are happy to have me."

Dauphine smiled widely, for the first time. She stepped up, hugged Alistair, and Alistair, surprised, hugged her back.

Dauphine finally pulled back and studied her with intensity.

"I hate my enemies with a great passion," Dauphine explained, "and I love my friends with equal fervor. You shall become a friend and a sister to me. A true sister. Anyone as devoted to Erec as you has won my heart. You shall find a loyal friend in me, I promise. And my word is greater than my bond."

Alistair felt that she meant it, and it felt so good to have a sister, to finally have the tension between them resolved. She could see that Dauphine was someone who felt deeply, and was not always able to control her passions.

"Will they give up?" Alistair asked, watching Bowyer's men.

Erec's mother shrugged.

"The Alzacs have always been separatists. They've always coveted the crown, and they are sore losers. My father and his father before him tried to eradicate them from the islands—now is the time. Without them, we shall be one nation, unified under Erec."

There came the sudden sound of a chorus of horns, and they all turned in alarm, looking up at the cliffs behind them. The mountaintops suddenly filled with soldiers on horseback, appearing all over the ridge, covering the horizon from all directions. Alistair saw them bearing all different color banners, and she looked up in confusion, not understanding what was happening.

"I don't understand," Alistair said. "The battle lies before us. Why do they approach from behind?"

Erec's mother's face fell with dread, and she looked as if she were watching the arrival of death itself.

"They are not for us," she said, her voice barely above a whisper. "Those banners—they have turned half the island against us. They are following Bowyer in his bid to be King. It's a revolt!"

"It is finished," Dauphine said, her voice filled with despondency. "We have been ambushed. Deceived."

"They head for the house of the sick," his mother observed, as the forces began to steer down the slope. "They're going to kill Erec—so that Bowyer can be King."

"We must stop them!" Alistair said.

Erec's mother grabbed Alistair's wrist.

"If you head forward, to Erec, you head to a certain death. If you wish to survive, head back to our forces, regroup, and live to fight another day."

Alistair shook her head.

"You don't understand," she replied. "Without Erec, I am not alive anyway."

Alistair tore her hand from her grip, and she turned and ran headlong into the oncoming army, toward certain death, ready to do whatever she had to to reach Erec first. If he was going to die, she would die at his side.

# CHAPTER TWENTY-THREE

Thorgrin sat in the small boat, joined by his Legion brothers and Indra and Matus, all of them rowing in the dead calm, lost in their thoughts as they peered out to the ocean. Thor rowed, encouraged, feeling his mother's bracelet vibrating on his wrist, sensing he was getting closer to his son. As he studied the waves, covered in mist, he could not see anything, yet he could feel his son somewhere out there, could sense he was close. Most of all, Thor sensed his son was alive, and that he needed him.

He rowed harder, as did the others, his muscles rippling, determined.

As they cut through the water, slowly bobbing in the current, unable to see far beyond, Thor's thoughts turned to Mycoples and Ralibar, and he missed more than ever having the opportunity to soar through the sky, to simply ride on the back of a great beast, to see the world spread out below, to cover so much ground so quickly. Now he was confined to the earth, like any other human, traveling slowly, his sight hindered. He also missed the companionship of Mycoples dearly; it was as if a part of him had been killed back there.

Reece, beside him, took a break and clasped Thor's shoulder.

"We shall find Guwayne," he encouraged. "Or we shall all die trying."

Thor nodded back with equal solemnity, grateful for Reece's support. As Thor studied the waters, he wondered what would happen if he was all wrong, and if it was already too late. What if, when he finally found Guwayne, he was dead? Thor would be unable to live with himself. And he would be unable to break the news to Gwen.

Or what if, even worse, he *never* found him?

Thor tried to shake these thoughts from his mind as he rowed harder, knowing failure was not an option. He felt the bracelet vibrating, and he knew he needed to have faith. He did not know where they were going, but he realized that was all part of the test:

sometimes one needed to proceed on faith. Sometimes, faith was all one had. And sometimes tests came to make your faith stronger.

One hour blurred into the next as morning turned to afternoon, and Thor began to lose all sense of space and time, rowing and rowing, no sound in his ears but that of the oars lapping the water. The others began to slow their rowing, breathing hard, needing a break.

Every muscle in his body on fire, feeling on the point of collapse, Thor closed his eyes and slowed his rowing, too. He focused, tried to find his inner power, begged it to help direct him to his son.

*Please, Mother,* he thought. *If you're there, give me a sign. A clear sign. Please. For Guwayne's sake. I need your help.*

A screech tore through the air and Thor craned back his neck, and in the distance, he spotted Estopheles, circling high, producing a cry that filled the lonely ocean. She swooped down and dropped an object from her claw, and it plummeted down to the sea, landing in the water beside Thor. Water splashed up at him as it did, and Thor looked down, amazed, to see a small, glass bottle floating in the water.

He retrieved it, pulled out the cork, unrolled the scroll, and others gathered around as he read Gwendolyn's letter.

It touched Thor deeply, and he looked up the skies as Estopheles screeched, amazed to see her here, in the middle of nowhere, feeling less alone. He felt encouraged; he felt it was a sign, and that he would find Guwayne.

Estopheles suddenly turned in the other direction, and dove up and down repeatedly, and Thor sensed she was telling him something. That she was leading them somewhere.

Guwayne.

"We must follow her!" Thor called out to the others.

The wind suddenly picked up, the sails were filled, and they all turned the boat, heading toward Estopheles.

They sailed through a thick cloud of mist, hanging low on the waters, and when finally they emerged from the other side, Thor's heart pounded with delight. He was amazed to see, hardly a hundred yards away, an island, larger than the last one, clearly inhabited, footprints all over the beach.

And as they got closer, sailing into the breaking waves, Thor looked out and saw on the sand something which made him feel faith in life again: beached on the shore was a small boat. And judging by its size, it was large enough to hold just a single person.

A boy.

*

Thor and the others moved quickly through the dense island jungle, Thor out of breath, heart pounding as he ran, the others by his side, fanning out, tracking the footsteps in the sand that led from the beach. It was clear that from the footsteps that someone had discovered the boat, had taken Guwayne, and Thor burned as he thought of it. Whoever it was, he would make them pay—if he was not already too late.

The jungle was so thick that Thor could barely see as he ran, scratched by branches and not caring. When it got too thick, Thor drew his sword and hacked at anything in his way as he sprinted with all he had, leaping over felled trees, hearing his heart pounding in his ears.

The sounds of exotic birds and animals punctuated the air, but Thor could barely hear anything other than his own heartbeat, than his own thoughts driving him mad. Where had they taken his boy? How long ago had he landed? Were they friendly, or did they have sinister intentions?

And worst of all: what if he did not find him in time?

His mother's bracelet buzzed like crazy, and Thor could barely think straight knowing that his son was here, just out of his reach, just out of reach, somewhere behind these trees.

"It looks like an army took him!" Matus yelled out, looking down as he ran.

Thor was thinking the same thing—there were so many tracks in so many different directions. How many people lived here? What sort of people were they? Where could they all be leading?

As they burst through a thick wall of foliage, there came the sudden sound of tribal chanting and dancing, a persistent drumbeat filling the air. The drums beat so fast, to the beat of Thor's heart, and they grew louder as he ran. They all ran for the direction of the music, and Thor felt both encouraged, and a sense of dread. Whoever was

152

out there did not sound friendly. Why, he wondered for the millionth time, would they take his son? What would they do with him?

"Do you know of the people of this isle?" Thor called out to Matus. "The Upper Isles is closer than the Ring."

Matus shook his head as he ran, dodging a tree.

"I've never been this far north. I didn't even know these islands were inhabited. Your guess is as good as mine."

They all came to a sudden stop at the edge of the jungle, right before a wall of vines, through which they could see a vast clearing. Hardened warriors, they all knew better than to rush through the perimeter of a hostile enemy without first taking stock.

Thor stared, breathing hard, and was amazed at the sight before him: in the clearing stood hundreds of natives, men with translucent white skin and bulging, glowing green eyes. They were barely clothed, and had wiry, muscular bodies. They chanted and beat on drums, dancing in circles every which way, again and again, circling barefoot on the sand in the jungle clearing. In the center of their village was a tall stone well, and above it, draped across, a thick log. Smoke rose from the well, and from inside it, Thor could hear screams.

A baby's screams.

The hairs stood on Thor's back as he listened, as he watched the natives circling, dancing around the well again and again, raising torches, banging on drums. He realized, with a flash of horror, what was happening: these primitive people were getting ready to sacrifice that baby.

Without even thinking of a strategy, without even considering how outnumbered they were, Thor burst into the clearing, sword drawn, and raised a great battle cry, charging these hundreds of armed warriors. Even if he had stopped to think of it, Thor would not have paused; something visceral inside of him drove him forward. Thor knew that could be his son in that well, and he would kill anyone and anything in his path to rescue him.

His brothers all joined him, all of them rushing headlong into danger, all by his side, prepared to go anywhere with him, no matter what the risk.

They had hardly gone ten feet, were still a good fifty yards away, when the entire village spotted them, and hundreds of warriors stopped their dancing and turned toward them. They raised their spears, and bows and arrows, and charged to meet them.

Thor did not slow, and neither did his brothers. The seven of them raced headlong into the army, reckless and carefree, preparing to do battle to the death.

They all met each other in a clash of arms. Thor, sword held high, was the first to reach them. Three tribesmen raised crude daggers and leapt for him, and as they did, Thor ducked low, and slashed, slicing their chests and sending them all collapsing to the ground, as he rolled out of the way.

Thor jumped back to his feet and continued his charge, heading for a group of tribesmen who were all raising spears, preparing to throw them right at him. Thor leapt into the air and sliced the spears in half before they could throw them, then he planted his sword in the ground and used it to propel himself into the air, swinging his legs around and kicking them all in the chest and knocking them back. Thor landed back on his feet, grabbed his sword, and swung around in a wide circle, felling them all.

Thor heard the baby's cry in the distance, ringing in his ears, rising even above the shouts of the men, and he fought like a man possessed. He did not try to summon his powers; he did not want to. He wanted to kill these men with his bare hands, these men who dared take his son from him, who dared try to kill him. He wanted to kill them all man to man, face to face.

Thor slashed left and right as these men came at him with daggers and spears. Thor killed them left and right, but he could not kill all of them before they fired off at him. One of the tribesmen hurled a stone with his sling, and it hit Thor hard in the head, cutting him above his temple and drawing blood. Others fired off arrows before Thor could reach them, and while Thor ducked and evaded most, seeing them coming from the corner of his eye, he could not miss all of them, and one arrow grazed his left arm. He cried out in pain as it drew blood.

Yet still Thor did not slow down. He thought of nothing but his child, and even with his wounds, Thor continued to charge, swinging his sword with both hands, slashing and kicking and elbowing his way for the village center. Soon he was engulfed by tribesmen, elbow to elbow with them, fighting hand to hand, eye to eye, through the thick crowd. It was slow going, even with his brothers fighting side by side with him, helping to block blows and felling tribesmen in their own right.

Thor was faster and stronger than these natives with their crude weapons, and he weaved in and out of them expertly, dodging spear thrusts as he slashed and stabbed. Yet the crowd grew thick, and there were just too many of them, and as he found himself enclosed from all sides, there were a few he never saw coming. Thor heard something behind him, and spun to see a villager lowering his dagger for the back of his head. It was too late to react, and Thor braced himself for the blow.

Suddenly, the tribesman opened his eyes wide and collapsed at Thor's feet, and Thor watched him fall, puzzled. He looked down and saw an arrow through his back, and he looked up to see O'Connor, holding his bow, grinning, his aim as true as always. Indra stood beside him and fired off an arrow of her own, and as she did, Thor heard a grunting noise and he looked over to see another tribesman, to his right, fall before he could unleash his spear.

Elden stepped forward, wielding a huge hammer, and in a broad stroke, he knocked three of them across the chest with a thumping noise, sending them to the ground. Elden then raised his hammer and turned it sideways, and butted two of them across the face, knocking them down. He then swung the heavy hammer over his head and sent it sailing into the mass of bodies, and it took down four more tribesmen, creating a path in the crowd.

Reece lunged forward with his sword, slashing every which way, while Conven did not even bother swinging his sword as he ran recklessly right into the thick of the tribesmen. He reached up and snatched a spear from one of their hands, and used that spear against its own attacker. He then spun around, creating a circle around him as he slashed every which way, downing tribesmen left and right. When he was done, Conven raised it above his head and hurled it with such force that it went through one tribesman and into another.

As Thor made progress, fighting his way through the crowd, his shoulders burning from the nonstop battle, he heard a whooshing noise above his head, and he noticed Matus coming up beside him, swinging a spiked flail, the chain swishing through the air as the metal ball found its target again and again, taking down a half dozen of them and lightening the crowd.

Thor, freed up, emboldened by all his brothers at his side, slashed deeper into the crowd, forging his way, keeping an eye on the distant well, hearing the baby's screams, watching the tribesmen standing menacingly above it. Thor noticed one of them nod to the other and then saw them begin to turn a crank, and lower the screaming baby down toward the fire.

Desperate, Thor stabbed a tribesman in the chest, snatching a spear from his hands, yanked it backwards, then took a step forward and threw it.

The spear sailed through the air, above the heads of the others, and finally, Thor, with his perfect aim, killed one of the tribesmen turning the cranks. O'Connor, picking up on his lead, fired off an arrow himself, and hit the other tribesman between the eyes. They both fell off the edge of the well, dead.

Determined to reach his son, Thor fought twice as hard, cutting his way through like a man possessed. Something came over him, a supreme rage beyond which he could control, and Thor leaned back and let out an unearthly shriek, veins popping in his arms and neck and shoulders, the sound of a desperate creature determined to rescue its young.

Thor moved with the speed of lightning, a one-man killing machine, as he cut through the rest of the men, creating a one-man warpath of destruction. The tribesmen were helpless against a warrior such as he, a warrior unlike any they had encountered before. This was the fight of Thor's life, and he would stop at nothing to achieve his goal.

Within moments, Thor cut a path through them, a pile of bodies lining up through the crowd's center. It was like he had entered a gap in space and time, and he was not fully conscious of what he was doing, or even where he was. He was taken over by the killing.

Thor reached the village center, and he wiped the sweat from his eyes, trying to understand what had just happened to him. He had felt the power of a hundred men, even if just for a moment, and he had been invincible.

The baby's cries snapped Thor back to the present, and he quickly turned and raced for the stone well.

With no one left between him and the well, Thor scrambled to climb to the top of it, as sweat stung his eyes, his heart pounding.

*Please, God. Let my son be alive.*

As Thor reached the top, the cries grew louder, echoing in the empty well, and he coughed and gagged from the rising smoke. Thor reached down and with shaking hands yanked at the crank, again and again, the rope rising, turning, raising up the baby as Thor rescued it from the heat and the smoke.

Thor pulled and pulled, anxious to see that the baby was okay, and as it finally reached the top, Thor reached down in the smoke and held the baby, lifting it up, and turned to look into his son's eyes.

Thor was elated to see that the baby was alive and healthy. Yet as he examined the baby, naked, lying in the bassinet, Thor was shocked to discover something: it was not his son.

It was a girl.

The girl screeched as Thor held her high. He was glad to have saved her. But it was not his son. It was someone else's child.

Indra and the others reached the top of the well, beside Thor, and as they did, Thor handed the baby to her, then immediately turned and scanned the village, looking for any sign of his son. From up here he had a great perspective, and could see the whole village spread out below. The rest of his brothers were finishing off the last of the tribesmen, and all of them were dead, bodies sprawled out everywhere.

But nowhere was there any sign of Guwayne.

Thor was determined to get answers. On the far side of the village he saw one villager, wounded, slowly getting to his feet, and he leapt down off the wall, racing for him as he tried to crawl away.

Thor jumped on his back, pinned him down to the sand with one knee, drew a dagger, and turned the man over and held it to his throat.

"Where is my baby?" Thor demanded, eyes bulging with panic and rage.

The man mumbled something in a language Thor could not understand, panic in his eyes.

Thor, desperate, tightened the blade against the man's throat.

"MY BABY!" Thor shrieked, turning and pointing at Indra, who held the screaming baby girl.

The villager finally seemed to understand, and he mumbled something again.

"I don't understand!" Thor yelled.

The man suddenly turned and pointed up, over Thor's shoulder.

Thor turned and followed his finger, and he saw a distant mountain range, and near the top, winding its way up, a small procession of men. They were heading towards the top of the volcano, and in their center, raised above their heads, was a small case, born on poles, gleaming gold, shining in the sun.

A case just large enough to hold a baby.

# CHAPTER TWENTY-FOUR

Gwen ran through the ship, panic-stricken as she watched her people turning to stone, one after the next, and falling over the rail, into the water. It was like something out of her worst nightmare. Quickly, she was losing her ranks, the thousands of survivors of the Ring piled onto three ships, quickly thinning out.

Gwen saw Steffen about to look over the edge, and she ran to him, grabbed him by the back of his shirt, and yanked him backwards. He went stumbling and landed on his rear, and he looked up at her in shock.

"Don't look!" she cried. "You'll be killed."

Shock gave way to gratitude, as he realized. He stood and bowed before her.

"My lady," he said, eyes welling with tears, "you saved my life."

"Help me save others," she replied.

Steffen rushed about to help the others, and he was joined by Sandara, Kendrick, Godfrey, Brandt and Atme, along with the new Legion members, Merek and Ario, all of them racing with Gwendolyn throughout the ship, saving people from looking over the edge, preventing people from getting too close to loved ones who had already turned to stone and were plummeting. Gwen watched a wife shriek as her husband had just turned to stone. She watched him clutch his body, refusing to let go, trying to keep him from falling over the edge, and then she herself inevitably looking over at the water. She, too, turned to stone, her face frozen in a look of agony, and together, her arms wrapped around him, as one big chunk of stone, they fell over the edge and plunged into the deep.

Gwen looked out at her other two ships and was horrified to see that one of them was now completely empty, all of the people on board having turned to stone and plummeted over. The railings were all broken from where the stones had smashed them, and there remained not a sole survivor left. In fact, as all the stones begin to pile up on one side of the ship, the ship itself began to list, and as Gwen watched, helpless, it began to sink.

The ship sank with increasing speed, and in moments it landed on its side in the water with a great splash, its sails smacking against the ocean. It lay on its side, bobbing, all its people dead before it even capsized, and Gwen felt sick to her stomach as she saw it sink completely into the water below.

Gwen could hardly believe that there now remained but two ships of the glorious fleet that had once set out from the Ring. Gwen looked about frantically, fearing she would lose all of her people here.

"Raise the masts!" she yelled to her admiral. "Double the men on the oars! Get us away from these waters!"

Men broke into action as bells sounded, taking positions, doing their best to move the ships along.

Gwen rushed to Sandara and grabbed her wrist, desperate for answers.

"How long will these waters last?" she asked.

Sandara shook her head grimly.

"They travel on the open ocean, my lady," she said. "These waters are like a school of fish, passing through. I've never encountered them myself, but I've heard they pass quickly—especially with a strong wind."

Gwen turned and peered out at the distant horizon, keeping her eyes up high, afraid to look down at the waters. It was hard to tell where they ended.

She turned and craned her neck and looked back up at the sails and was relieved to see them hoisted, and filled with a good wind. Men grunted all about her as they rowed and rowed.

"They might pass quickly," Gwen said, "but we shall take no chances. You will all row until the tomorrow breaks!"

Gwen looked up, saw the sun at high noon, and knew it would be a long, backbreaking day for them all. But she would take no chances. It was still better than death.

Gwendolyn found Illepra, holding the baby, sheltering her, and Gwen's heart soared in relief as she took her back. On the silent, somber air, all that could be heard was the lapping of the oars against the water, the cries of the gulls, and the soft moaning and sobbing of the survivors, heartbroken, mourning loved ones. They were the lucky ones. But Gwen did not feel lucky.

Indeed, as she looked out at the horizon and considered their meager rations, she knew this did not bode well. It did not bode well at all.

*

Gwendolyn, bleary-eyed, sat up and watched as dawn broke over the ocean, a thin purple line blending to scarlet, burning the mist off the ocean. A lone gull cried up above, and as the sky warmed, Gwen turned and surveyed her people: they were all bent over their oars, sleeping in place, exhausted from their efforts. It had been a long and harrowing day and night, and Gwen had thought it would never end. She had handed the baby to Illepra late in the night and had finally fallen asleep.

As the sun began to creep over the horizon, Gwendolyn, who had stayed awake all night, rose and took the first steps, the only one awake on the quiet ship. She made her way gingerly to the rail, the deck creaking as she went, and braced herself to look over, to examine the waters. She wanted to be the first to look, the first to know for sure that the waters were safe. She didn't feel it was right to have one of her subjects test it. She was Queen, after all, and if someone were to die, it should be her. She felt it was her responsibility.

Gwen crossed the deck, and just as she reached the rail, a voice cut through the still morning air:

"My lady."

Gwen turned and saw Steffen standing there, dark circles beneath his eyes, looking back at her with concern.

"I fear I know where you are going," he said, his voice filled with worry.

Gwen nodded back.

"I will check the waters," she replied.

Steffen shook his head and stepped forward.

"That is no job for a Queen," he said. "I am your servant. Allow me to check."

He began to walk forward, for the rail, but Gwen reached out and laid a hand on his wrist.

He turned to her.

"Thank you," she said. "But no. It is my ship, my people. It is for me to check."

His brow furrowed.

"My lady, you could die."

"So can you. And who is to say my life is worth more than yours?"

Steffen's eyes watered over as he looked back at her.

"You truly are a great Queen," he said. "A Queen like no other."

Gwen could hear how much he meant it, and it touched her.

Without further ado, Gwen turned, took two big steps to the rail, clutched it with trembling hands and closed her eyes, images flashing through her mind of all the people who had turned to stone. She prayed she did not meet the same fate.

Gwen opened her eyes and looked over, taking a deep breath and bracing herself.

The waters, lit by the morning sun, were glowing blue. Gwen looked carefully, and she was elated to see no trace of the lightened waters. The sea was back to the way it had been.

"My lady!" Steffen called out in alarm, rushing forward to his side.

Gwen smiled as she turned and calmly looked back at him.

"I'm alive," she said. "There is nothing more to fear."

All around her, Gwen's people began to rise, getting to their feet, bleary-eyed. One by one, they looked at her in awe, then made their way over to her.

"The waters are safe!" Gwen called out.

The people cried out with relief, and as one they all rushed to the edge of the rail, leaned over and examined the sea in wonder. It was just a normal ocean, like it had always been.

Gwendolyn was struck with a hunger pang, and she thought of their dwindling rations and wondered when her people had last eaten. She herself had abstained two meals a day, to save more for her people, and she was starting to feel the hunger. She was almost afraid to ask what remained.

She turned to her admiral, who stood beside her, and she could see from the grim look on his face that it was not good.

"The rations?" she asked, hesitant.

He shook his head gravely.

"I am sorry, my lady," he reported. "There is nothing left."

"The people clamor for food," Aberthol added, beside her. "They are growing desperate. They rowed throughout the night, and now they have nothing. I do not know how much longer we shall be able to appease them."

"Or how much longer we will be able to survive," Brandt added, grimly.

Gwendolyn took in the news, feeling the weight of it. She turned to Kendrick, who stood beside her.

"And what do you propose we do?" Gwendolyn asked.

He shook his head.

"If we do not find provisions soon," he said, "if we do not find land soon, this ship shall become a floating grave."

Gwendolyn turned to Sandara, standing beside him.

"How much farther until we reach your land?" she asked Sandara.

Sandara shook her head and looked out and studied the horizon.

"It is hard to say, my lady," she said. "It depends on the currents. It could be a day—or it could be a month."

Gwen's stomach tightened at her words. A month. Her people would not survive. They would all die here, waste away, an awful death in the midst of the ocean. Worse, they would surely turn on each other, revolt, and kill one another. Hunger could make people desperate.

Gwendolyn nodded, resigned.

"Let us pray for land," she said.

# CHAPTER TWENTY-FIVE

Darius walked quickly through his village as the sun began to set, more nervous than he'd ever been, repeatedly wiping the sweat from his palms. He could not understand why he was so anxious as he weaved his way, heading toward the river, to meet Loti at her cottage. He had faced brothers in combat, had labored under taskmasters, had even been engaged in the most dangerous of toil in the mines, and yet he had never felt nervous like this before.

Yet as Darius headed to meet Loti, he felt his mind buzzing, his heart pounding, and he could not keep his throat from going dry. He could not understand how she had this effect over him, what it was about her. He barely even knew her, had only laid eyes upon her twice, and yet now, as he headed to meet her, he could think of little else.

Darius thought back to their encounter, and he turned over her words in his mind again and again. He tried to remember exactly what she had said; he was starting to doubt himself, starting to wonder if she really liked him, if she felt the same way about him as he did her, or perhaps whether she just wanted to see him in a casual way, or was just curious to know more about him. Perhaps she was dating someone else; perhaps she would stand him up and not even meet him at all.

Darius's heart beat faster as he considered all the scenarios. He had dressed himself in his best clothes: a white cotton tunic and black pants of fine wool, clothes his father had once worn. They were the best clothes his family owned, and his father had paid dearly for them. Still, as Darius examined them, he felt self-conscious about them, seeing how stained and torn they were in places, still the dress of a slave, even if slightly elevated. They were not the clothes of the Empire, not the clothes of a free man. Yet no one in his village had the clothes of a free man.

Darius finally emerged from the busy, winding village streets as he came to the western end of the village, a sprawling complex of small cottages built nearly on top of one another. As he searched the dwellings, he tried to remember what she had said: *a cottage with a door stained red*.

Darius went from house to house, looking everywhere, and just when he was about to give up, suddenly, his eyes settled on it. There it was, standing apart from the others, slightly smaller than the rest, looking exactly like the others except for the faded red stain on the door.

Darius gulped. He looked down and checked the flowers in his hand, wildflowers he had plucked from the side of the river bank, yellow, with long thin stems. He was sorry now that they weren't of a better quality; he should have picked the wild roses on the far side of the meadow, but he hadn't had time for that.

*Next time*, he told himself. *That is, if she even wants to see me again.*

Darius stepped up and knocked, and he could barely even take in what was happening, his heart slamming in his chest, drowning out all thoughts but its pounding. He could barely even hear the screams of the children, and all the villagers running chaotically about him, all drowned out as he knocked on the door.

Darius stood, waiting, and began to doubt whether it would ever open, or whether he was ever even truly invited here. Had he been mistaken? Had he imagined the whole thing?

Darius stood there so long that, finally, he turned to go—when the door suddenly opened. There appeared the face of an older woman, staring back at him suspiciously. She opened the door wide and stepped out, hands on her hips, and looked him up and down as if he were an insect. Her eyes fell on the flowers he held, and her face fell in disappointment.

"*You're* the one who's come to see my daughter?" she asked.

He stared back, silent, not knowing how to respond.

"And *those* are what you brought her?" she added, staring at the flowers.

Darius looked down at the flowers, panic welling up inside him.

"I…um…I am sorry—"

The woman was suddenly bumped aside as Loti appeared beside her, a broad smile on her face. She stepped up, took the flowers from Darius's hands and she examined them, delighted.

As she did, all of Darius's fears began to melt away. Loti looked more beautiful than he'd even remembered, freshly bathed, wearing beautiful white linen from head to toe, and he had never seen her smile—not like that.

"Oh, Mother, stop being so hard on him," Loti said. "These flowers are perfectly beautiful."

She fixed her eyes on Darius, and his heart beat faster.

"Well, are you coming in?" she asked, giggling, stepping forward and linking arms with him, and then leading him into her cottage, squeezing past her mother.

Darius entered the small, dark cottage, and she led him to a seat, against the far wall, hardly ten feet from the entrance. They sat side by side on a small clay bench, and her mother closed the door and came back inside, and sat across from them on a stool.

Her mother kept her eyes locked on Darius, examining him, and Darius felt claustrophobic in the small, dim cottage. He shifted in his chair. He realized it was the tradition of all the women in the village to interrogate him before allowing him to take her daughter anywhere. Out of respect for her parents, Darius wanted to make sure he did nothing to offend them. He was determined to make a good impression.

"You wish to see my daughter," the woman said, her expression hard. She had the face of a warrior, and Darius could see from her expression that she was a mother of sons—of warrior sons. It was the face of a cautious, protective mother, one determined not to repeat past mistakes.

"Your daughter is very beautiful," Darius finally said, his first words, not knowing what else to say.

She scowled.

"I know that she is," she said. "I don't need you to tell me she's beautiful. Anyone can see that. She has been desired by every boy in this village. You are not the first to seek her hand. Why should I let her spend any time with you?"

Darius's heart pounded as he tried to figure out what to say. He wanted to be respectful, but he was not willing to back down either.

"I will admit that I do not even know your daughter," he said slowly. "But I have witnessed her great strength of spirit and of courage. I admire her very much. That is the same strength of courage I hope to have in my wife, in the mother of my children. I would like to get to know her. I mean only the highest respect to you and to her."

Her mother stared at him long and hard, as if debating, her expression never changing.

"You speak well for your age," she finally said. "But I know who your father was. He was a rebel. An outcast. A warrior. A great man, but a reckless one. There is no room for heroics among our people. We are slave people. That is our lot. It will never change. *Ever*. Do you understand me?"

She stared at him long and hard in the thick silence, and Darius swallowed, not knowing what to say.

"I don't want my daughter with a hero," she said. "I've already lost one son learning that the Empire cannot be destroyed. I will not lose my daughter, too."

She stared at Darius, cold and hard, unyielding, waiting for an answer.

Darius wished he could tell her what she wanted to hear, that he would never fight the Empire, that he would be docile and complacent with his lot as a slave.

But deep down, it was not how he felt. He was not willing to lie down, and he did not want to lie to her.

"I admire my father," Darius said, "even though I barely knew him. I have no plan to attack the Empire. Nor can I promise you I will lie down in defeat my entire life. I am who I am. I can pretend to be no one else."

Her mother studied him, squinting her eyes in the interminable silence, and Darius felt sweat forming on his forehead in the small cottage, wondering if he had ruined his chances.

Finally, she nodded.

"At least you are honest," she said. "That is more than I can say for the other boys. And honesty counts a great deal."

"Great!" Loti said, suddenly standing. "We're done then!"

She grabbed Darius's arm, pulled him up and before he could react, led him out of the cottage, past her mother, to the open the door.

"Loti, I did not say we are done!" her mother cried out, standing.

"Oh, come on, Mother," Loti said. "The boy barely knows me. Give us a chance. You can attack him when we return."

Loti giggled as she opened the door; yet before they were halfway out, Darius felt a cold grip on his arm, squeezing his bicep, yanking him back.

He turned to see mother staring at him sternly.

"If anything happens to my daughter because of you, I guarantee you I will kill you myself."

*

Darius sat across from Loti in the small boat and he rowed down the slow-moving river on the outskirts of their village, bordered by marshland, following the route of this lazy river which circled the village. This river ran in a continuous circle, and it was a favorite among small kids, who would place small toy boats in it, release them, and wait for them to return on the current. It would take an entire day.

It was also a favorite among lovers. With its slow-moving current and idyllic breezes, the river was the best place to be at sunset, as the heat of the day dissipated and the wind picked up.

Darius had been delighted by the look on Loti's face when she saw where he had brought her. Finally, he felt as if he had done something right.

Now she leaned back in the boat and looked up at the sky as if she were in heaven, as Darius rowed them gently down the river. The current carried them, so he did not need to row much, and he rested his elbows on the oars and allowed the boat to be carried by its own weight. As they floated there in the silence, Darius thought of how lucky he was to be here, and of how beautiful Loti looked, her dark skin lighting up in the sunset.

Darius leaned forward and clasped his palm over the soft back of her hand, and she looked up, smiling. She still played with the flowers he had given her, and as her eyes met his, he had forgotten what he was going to say. She stared back at him, her eyes filled with intensity and passion, as if looking into his soul.

"Yes?" she asked.

Darius wanted to speak, but the words stuck in his throat. So they floated silently as he blushed, passing swaying marshes, lit up in the sunset, a beautiful amber and scarlet, rustling in the breeze.

"You're different from the others," she finally said. "I don't know what it is. But there's something about you. I can sense you are a warrior, yet I can also sense something else…I don't know, a sensitivity, maybe. As if you see things. As if you understand things. I like being with you. It sets me at ease."

Darius blushed as he looked down. Did she know about his powers? he wondered. Would she hate him for it? Would she tell the others?

"Most boys your age," she said, "are already with girls, or are already married. Not you. I've never seen you with others."

"I did not know you saw me at all," he said, surprised.

"I have eyes," she said. "You are a hard person to miss."

Darius blushed some more. He looked down at the boat and toed it with his foot. He did not know how to respond, so he kept silent. He had always been shy around girls; he did not have the natural talent for speech that other boys had. Yet he also felt things very deeply. He watched other boys be quick to find girls, and quick to toss them away when they were done with him. But Darius could never do that. Any girl he would be with he would take very seriously, and it had kept him back from committing to anyone. He felt too much at stake.

"And you?" Darius finally mustered the courage to ask. "You are not married either."

She stared back at him proudly.

"There is no shame in that," she said, defensive. "I make my own decisions. I do not follow my passions easily. I've turned away all those who have approached me."

Darius felt nervous at her words. Would she turn him away, too?

"Why?" he asked.

"I am waiting for someone remarkable," she said. "More than just a man; more than just a warrior. Someone who is special. Who is different. Who has a great destiny before him."

Darius was confused, and suddenly wondered if this whole trip was a waste.

"Then why are you sitting here with me?" he asked.

Loti laughed, and the sound of it, high-pitched and sweet, caught him off guard. When she finally stopped, her eyes, playful, settled on him.

"Maybe I have found it," she said.

They locked eyes for a moment, then they each looked away, embarrassed.

Darius began to row again, not quite understanding her yet also feeling a stronger connection with her. He didn't quite understand what she wanted, or what she saw in him. He was afraid he might lose her. He wanted to impress her somehow, to convince her to like him. But he didn't know what to say.

They continued floating down the river in silence, the air thick with the rustling of the marsh, with the sound of the breezes, with the night insects beginning to sing. Darius's muscles slowly relaxed, tired from a long day of labor. It was unusual for him to relax, to not be thinking of his work the next day, of his miserable existence, of craving a way out of here. For the first time in a long time, he was happy right where he was.

"Does it not bother you," he asked, "knowing that tomorrow when we arise, we'll be answering to someone else?"

Loti did not meet his eyes, but stared out in the distance and shrugged.

"Of course it bothers me," she finally replied. "But there are some things you must learn to live with it. I have learned to."

"I have not," he said.

She studied him.

"Your problem," she said, "is that you are narrow-minded. You only see one way to resist."

He looked back at her, puzzled.

"What other way is there to resist than to throw off the chains of our oppressors?" he asked.

She smiled back.

"The highest form of resistance is to enjoy life, even in the face of oppression. If you can find a way to live a life of joy in the face of danger, if you have not let them crush your spirit, then you have defeated them. They can affect our bodies, but not our spirit. If they can't take away your joy, then you are never oppressed. Oppression is a state of mind."

Darius pondered her words, never considering it that way before. He had never met anyone who thought like her, who saw the world the way she did. He not know if he agreed with her, but he could understand her way of thinking.

"I think we are very different people," he finally said.

"Maybe that is why we like each other," she replied.

His heart beat faster at her words, and he smiled back. For the first time, he felt relaxed, more confident.

Their boat rounded a bend, and as it did, she opened her eyes wide, and he turned to look. The current had taken them under the Tree of Fire, and as Darius turned and laid eyes on it, he was awestruck, as always. The tree, hundreds of feet high and wide, was as ancient as this land. Its branches leaned over the river, all the way down until they touched it, its leaves a flaming red, bright red flowers blooming at the end of them, and all aglow in the sunset. It looked magical. Darius could smell its strong fragrance from here, like cinnamon crossed with honeysuckle.

Darius stopped their boat beneath the branches, the flowers nearly touching their heads, emitting a soft glow as evening fell, lighting up the twilight. Loti leaned forward, so close that her knees were touching Darius's, and she reached up and placed a hand in his. He could feel her trembling, and as he looked into her eyes, his heart pounded.

"You are not like the others," she said. "I can see it in your eyes. I want to be with you."

Darius stared back at her, and could see the earnestness in her eyes.

"And I with you," he said.

"I do not give out my heart lightly," she said. "I do not want it broken."

"I promise it shall never be," he said.

Darius then leaned forward, and as his lips met hers, as he reached up and touched her face, as the two of them floated there, under the Tree of Fire, he felt, for the first time, that he had something to live for.

# CHAPTER TWENTY-SIX

Gwen stood at the rail, looking down into the waters, and she raised her hands to her eyes to shield them as a sudden light filled the sky. The haze hanging over the sea was infused with gold, and as she squinted into the light, she suddenly spotted something sailing toward her. She narrowed her eyes and wondered if she were seeing things: there, before her, bobbing in the waters, floated a small, shining golden boat, reflecting the sun. Gwen looked closely as it came closer, and her heart soared to see who was inside. She could not believe it.

There, inside, was Thor, standing, smiling triumphantly. And in his arms he held their baby.

Gwen's heart soared, as she burst into tears at the sight. There they were, just feet away, returned to her, both alive and safe and well.

Gwen turned for a moment to summon the others on her ship, to share the good news—yet as she did, she was confused to find her ship empty. She could not understand where everyone had gone.

Gwen stepped into the small lifeboat on deck and quickly lowered the ropes until she reached the water. As she touched down, her boat bobbed wildly in the waves, and the thick rope connecting her to the ship snapped.

Gwen craned her neck and looked up, and was horrified to see her ship floating away on the strong ocean tide.

Gwen turned back to Thor and Guwayne, and she was horrified to see that her boat was suddenly getting sucked away, faster and faster on the tides, bringing her farther from them.

"NO!" she called out.

Gwen reached out a hand for Thorgrin, who still stood there, smiling, holding Guwayne. But the ocean tide carried her faster and farther away from him, away from her ship, away from everything she knew, deep into the limitless ocean.

Gwen awoke with a start. She looked all around, breathing hard, sweating, wondering what had happened. She saw that she was still in her ship; that she lay on deck; that it was filled with people. It had all been a nightmare. Just an awful, cruel nightmare.

Gwen's relief quickly morphed to disappointment as she saw the state of her people. A thick fog settled in over everything, carried on the wind, and Gwen could only see her people piecemeal. But she saw them slumped over their oars, lying curled up on the deck, leaning against the side rail, all of them languid, no one moving. She could tell right away that they had all been devastated by hunger. They all lay there, motionless, looking more dead than alive.

Gwen did not know how many days they had been floating here; she could no longer remember. She knew it was long enough, though. Too long. Land had never come, and here her people lay, all on the steps of death.

Gwendolyn felt hunger pains tear through her body, and it took all her might just to pull herself up to a sitting position. She sat there, holding the baby, who cried as Gwen gave her a bottle empty of milk. Gwen felt like weeping, but she was too exhausted for that. After all they been through, after having come so far, it killed her to think that now her people were all going to die here, in the middle of nowhere, from hunger. It was too much to take. For herself, she could suffer; but she hated to see her people suffer like this.

Gwen could sense the stale odor of death in the air, feel that this ship had become a floating tomb, and that, soon, they would all be dead. She could not help but feel as if it were all her fault.

"Do not blame yourself, my lady," came the voice.

Gwen turned to see her brother, Kendrick, sitting not far away, smiling weakly back. He must have read her thoughts, as he often did growing up, as he sat there, so noble, with such a strength of spirit, even at a time of such hardship.

"You have been a remarkable Queen," he said. "Our father would be proud. You've taken us further than anyone else could have dared hope. It is a miracle we lived this long."

Gwen appreciated his kind words, yet still, she could not help but feel responsible.

"If we all die, what have I done?" she asked.

"We will all die one day," he replied. "You have achieved honor. That is far more than we could have asked of ourselves."

Kendrick reached out a reassuring hand, and Gwen took it, grateful for his always being there.

"I should think you would have been a better King than I a Queen," she said. "Father should have chosen you."

Kendrick shook his head.

"Father knew what he was doing," he said. "He chose perfectly. It was the one great choice of his life. He chose you not for the good times—but for a time like this. He knew you would lead us out."

Before she could ponder his words, Gwen heard a shuffling of feet, and she turned and looked over to see Steffen looking down at her, dark circles under his eyes, looking weak, Arliss at his side, holding his hand.

Steffen cleared his throat.

"My lady, I have never made a request of you," he said, his voice weak, "but I have one now."

She looked at him, surprised, wondering what it could be.

"Whatever it is that I can grant, you shall have it," she replied.

"Would you stand as witness between us?" he asked. "We wish to marry."

Gwen stared back at them both, eyes wide in surprise.

"Marry?" she repeated, stunned. "Here, now?"

Steffen and Arliss nodded back, and Gwen could see the seriousness in their eyes.

"If not now, when?" Arliss asked. "None of us expect to make land. And before we die, we wish to be together, forever."

Gwen looked back at them both, overwhelmed by their devotion to each other. It made her think of Thorgrin, of her unfulfilled desire to wed him.

Her eyes filled with tears.

"Of course I shall," she replied.

Kendrick, Godfrey and the others close by who had overheard, all managed to muster to their feet and to join Gwen as she accompanied Steffen and Arliss to the bow of the ship.

Steffen and Arliss stood beside the rail, held hands, and turned and smiled to each other. Gwen stood before them, looking out at the fog, which rolled in and out on the silent ship, and she admired their courage, their affirmation of life in the midst of these dying moments.

"Do you have vows you wish to exchange?" Gwen asked.

Steffen nodded. He cleared his throat as he looked into Arliss's eyes.

"I, Steffen, vow to love you always," he said, "to be a faithful husband, and to remain at your side, whether in this life or the next, whatever the fates may bring."

Arliss smiled back at him.

"And I, Arliss, vow to love you always, to be a devoted wife, and to remain at your side, whether in this life or the next, whatever the fates may bring."

They leaned in and kissed, and as they did, Gwen noticed tears running down Arliss's cheek. It was a sacred moment, and a somber one; it was a moment when they all looked death in the face, and tried to beat it with their love.

It was an eerie affair, at once both the gloomiest wedding Gwendolyn had ever attended, and the most beautiful, all of them, Gwen realized, floating into nowhere, and as fleeting as the fog that rolled in and out with each passing wave. More than ever, Gwen felt death coming—and she felt lucky she had been alive long enough to witness, at least, one wedding of those she loved.

# CHAPTER TWENTY-SEVEN

Alistair sat inside Erec's chamber in the royal house of the sick, beside Dauphine and Erec's mother, along with a half dozen guards, standing before the door, two feet thick, bolted with sliding iron bars. Alistair sat beside Erec, who still lay sleeping, and held his hand, closing her eyes. She tried to drown out the cheering of the crowd outside, muted behind the stone walls two feet thick, a crowd whipped into a frenzy. It was obvious from the noise that they had been routed, that Bowyer had succeeded in his coup, and that they were cut off, encircled. Bowyer, she knew, would never let them go until Erec was dead and he was King.

Alistair, luckily, had reached Erec's chamber before the soldiers, barring the doors, insisting on being here by Erec's side. She looked down at Erec now, and she felt fresh tears roll down her face as she kissed the back of his hand. He was sleeping sweetly, as she knew he would be—with the healing spell she had cast on him, he would not rise for quite some time. When he did, he would still be in a weakened state, in no state to fight these men. She was on her own now.

Given her own weakened state, having used all of her precious energy to heal him, Alistair, try as she did, could not summon any magical powers to help her. She wished now that she had Thor by her side, or any warriors of the Ring, any of the Silver, who she knew would lay down their lives to save Erec. She found it ironic that, now that Erec was here, home with his own people, he was most in danger.

Alistair closed her eyes and focused.

*Mother, please help me.*

She kept her eyes closed tight, recalling all the dreams she'd had of her mother, of her high up on the cliff, in that castle, feeling her with her. She prayed and prayed.

But nothing came but silence.

Outside, there came a sudden pounding on the door, insistent. It felt like a pounding on her heart.

Alistair rose, crossed the room, and stood by the door. She glanced at Erec's mother, and Dauphine, who looked back at her in alarm.

"It's over," Dauphine said. "Now not only will my brother die, but we shall die with him. We should have taken flight when we had the chance."

"Then Erec would be dead," Alistair replied.

Dauphine shook her head.

"Erec will die anyway. Three women cannot stop an army. But if we had fled, we could have survived to assemble our own men for vengeance."

Alistair shook her head.

"If Erec dies, vengeance does not mean a thing. If he dies, I die with him."

"You might just get your wish," his mother said.

The pounding on the door came again and again, until it finally stopped and one distinct voice rang out above all others.

"Alistair, we know you are in there," boomed the voice.

Alistair recognized it immediately as Bowyer's. He sounded so close, yet so far away, the door so thick, there was no way he could knock it down.

"Bring him out to us," Bowyer continued, "and you shall all live. Keep him in there, and you will die with him. We cannot break down these doors, but we will trap you in. You will sit there, for days, and you will starve a painful death. There is no way out. Hand Erec to us and we shall grant you pardon and send you on the sea back to your homeland. I will not make this gracious offer twice."

Alistair stared at the door, seething, burning with the indignity of it all. They had caught her at a vulnerable moment, and now, as they knew, she was helpless.

But she would not give up on Erec. Not now. Never.

"If it is a murder you want," she boomed back, "if a life needs to be taken, then take mine!"

There came a murmur from the other side.

"Alistair, what are you saying?" his mother asked. But Alistair ignored her.

"By your own laws," she continued, "without a Queen, a King cannot be King—so if you take my life, you shall render Erec

177

powerless. Kill me, and become King yourself. My life for his. That is the only deal I shall offer."

There came a long silence, and a murmur on the other side of the door, until finally, Bowyer's voice boomed again: "Agreed!" he called out. "Your life for Erec's!"

Alistair nodded, satisfied.

"Agreed!" she called out.

Alistair took a deep breath, braced herself, and stepped forward, reaching for the iron bolt—and as she did, she felt a hand on her wrist.

She turned to see Erec's mother standing there, her eyes welling with tears.

"You don't need to do this," she said softly.

Alistair's teared up, too.

"My life to me is not half as important as Erec's," she said. "I can think of no better way to die than to die for him."

Erec's mother wept as Alistair stepped forward and the guards gently pulled his mother back. She pulled back the heavy iron bolt, the sound reverberating in the stone room, and swung open the thick door.

Alistair found herself facing Bowyer, glaring back, standing but a few feet away. Behind him stood hundreds of soldiers holding weapons, a sea of hostile faces. They all grew quiet, shocked at Alistair's presence.

Alistair stepped boldly through the open door, right for them, and they all parted ways and took a step back, as she walked right up to Bowyer. She stood there, a foot away from him, their eyes locked, each defiant.

There came the sound of the heavy doors slamming shut behind her, the bolt sliding back into place. She was now all alone out here, but she took comfort in the fact that Erec was safe inside.

"You are braver than I thought," Bowyer finally said in the long, thick silence. "Your courage will lead to your death."

Alistair stared back, calm and expressionless, unable to be shaken.

"Death is fleeting," she replied. "Courage is eternal."

They locked eyes and Alistair could see in Bowyer's expression, hidden beneath the anger, a look of awe.

Alistair held her hands out before her, and several soldiers rushed forward and bound them with ropes. There came a cheer from the crowd, as she felt herself pushed from behind, led past the cheering crowd, following the torchlit street into the cold black night, on her way to her execution.

# CHAPTER TWENTY-EIGHT

Romulus stood at the bow of his ship, hands on hips, and stared out at the looming shores of the Empire, and felt mixed feelings. On the one hand, he had been, in a sense, victorious, having done what Andronicus and no other Empire commander had ever been able to do—conquer and occupy the Ring. It was a feat that none of his predecessors could accomplish, and for that, he felt he should be celebrated, a returning hero. After all, now there was not a dot left on earth that did not belong to the Empire.

On the other hand, his wars had cost him dearly—too dearly. He had embarked from the Empire with a hundred thousand ships, and now he returned with a fleet of but three. He felt rage and humiliation at the thought of it. He knew he had Thorgrin to blame, whatever mysterious power he held, and of course that rebellious girl, Gwendolyn. Romulus vowed to one day capture and flay them both alive. He would make them pay for forcing him to return in humiliation to his homeland.

Romulus knew that, any way he tried to spin it, his returning with only three ships was a show of weakness. It left him vulnerable to revolt, and he knew that his first order of business would be to restore his fleet immediately. Which was why he had sailed here, first, to this northern city, to Volusia, before making his grand return to the Southern capital. He would replenish his fleet, and then return with all the pageantry he could muster. He would need it to consolidate the Empire. He looked about and saw the hundreds of gleaming ships in the harbor and knew that for the right price, any of them were for sale.

Volusia. Romulus looked out and studied this city by the sea as the tides pulled his meager three ships into the harbor, and he felt a fresh wave of resentment. The northern provinces of the Empire had always felt superior, had always reluctantly followed the commands of the Southern capital. It was an uneasy alliance, subject to flare ups every dozen years. Volusia, in Romulus's mind, should have been complacent and quick to obey, like all other Empire provinces;

instead, it was filled with the overly rich and indulgent leaders of the northern hemisphere, and ruled by that awful old Queen, with whom he had clashed more than once. Romulus could think of nothing he could despise more than having to see her ugly face while he haggled with her over buying a fleet of ships. He knew of her greed, and he had come prepared, his holds filled with gold. He hated being in this position of weakness.

Even worse, Romulus glanced up at the sky, saw no trace of the moon, and worried for the millionth time about that sorcerer's spell. His moon cycle was over, his period of invincibility had ended, and that, more than anything, terrified Romulus, left him feeling weak and vulnerable. He opened and closed his fists, flexed his muscles, and as he did, he felt no less weak, still felt the strength rippling through his muscles. He had no dragons left to do his bidding, but that did not matter now. The dragons were dead, and while he did not have them, no one else did, either. He had been a great warrior all his life, he reminded himself, even without the spell, and he saw no reason why, being back to his old self, he would be vulnerable.

Romulus tried not to think of the sorcerer's words, of his agreeing to that grand bargain, of giving up his soul to a dark devil in return for the moon cycle of strength he had been granted. Perhaps if he returned to that sorcerer's cave, he would grant him another cycle of power. And if not, perhaps if Romulus killed the man, that would end his bargain. Romulus warmed up at the thought—yes, perhaps killing the man would be the best route after all.

Romulus, feeling optimistic again, shaking off his fears, looked out at the approaching city, and he smiled for the first time. The Queen might have the advantage now, might take all his gold, but he would get his ships. And once he had them, he would return to this place, this city on the sea, when they least expected it, and set it to fire. First he would murder every last one of them. He would take back all of his gold and use it to create an immense, golden statue of himself, standing at the shore, and pointing at the sea.

Romulus smiled wide, happy at the thought. This would shape up to be a great morning after all.

Trumpets sounded all up and down the harbor, and Romulus saw Volusia's troops lining up on all sides, dressed in their finest, standing at attention, waiting to greet him. This was the sort of welcome he deserved. He knew they feared and respected the Southern capital, and yet Romulus couldn't recall Volusia welcoming him so warmly in the past. Perhaps these people had changed their tune, and had decided to step in line; perhaps they feared him more than he realized. Maybe, he thought, he would not burn down the city after all. Maybe he would just rape their women and steal their gold.

Romulus grinned as he imagined it in great detail, as their ship pulled up to the harbor, dozens of troops casting out gold-plated plank to his ship, as his men anchored their ship.

Romulus marched across it, strutting proudly, pleased at the welcome he was receiving, realizing that it would be easier than he thought to get the ships he needed. Perhaps they had heard of his conquest of the Ring, and had realized he was supreme leader after all.

Romulus stepped onto the docks, and dozens of soldiers parted ways, bowing their heads in respect. Romulus looked up and saw in the center of the crowd, hoisted up on a carriage of shining gold, the leader of Volusia. Her carriage was lowered, and Romulus expected to see the wrinkled old woman he had last seen years ago.

He was shocked to see a young, strikingly gorgeous girl, looking to be hardly eighteen years of age, staring back at him. She looked strikingly like the former Queen.

Romulus was completely caught off guard, something which rarely happened to him, as he stared back at this girl who stepped down off her carriage and walked proudly up to him, flanked by dozens of her soldiers. She stood but a few feet away, and stared at him without speaking. As he studied her features carefully, Romulus realized that she could be no other than the former Queen's daughter.

He suddenly flared up with anger, realizing he was being slighted by the Queen, sending out her daughter to greet him.

"Where is your mother?" Romulus demanded, indignant.

The girl remained poised, though, and stared back calmly.

"My mother of whom you speak is long dead," she replied. "I have killed her."

Romulus was shocked at her words, and even more so, by how deep, dark, and forceful her voice was. He studied her, caught off guard by her strong tongue, by her confident manner, by her deep, dark voice, by her sinister black eyes, and by her beauty. She wielded it like a weapon. He'd never encountered such strength before, male or female, in any commander, citizen, sorcerer—anyone. She was like an ancient warrior trapped in a young girl's body.

As Romulus studied her, slowly, he smiled wide, recognizing a kindred soul. She had killed her mother, no doubt had ruthlessly seized power for herself, and he admired that greatly. He made a mental note to find some pretext to stay the night here in this capital. He would feast with her. And when she least expected it, he would attack her, and have his fill of her.

"And what is your name, my dear princess?" he asked, taking a step forward, standing straighter, flexing his chest muscles, glistening in the sun, getting uncomfortably close to her so that she could understand the power and might of the Great Romulus.

She smiled back, and she surprised him: instead of backing away, as most people would, she stepped up closer to him.

"It is one you shall never forget," she said, whispering in his ear.

Romulus felt his skin tingling as she came closer, and he gawked at her beauty, his entire body flushing at the sight of her. Already, he realized, she was throwing herself at him—it would make tonight even easier.

"And why is that?" he asked.

She leaned in even closer, her soft, sensual lips brushing his ear.

"Because it is the last word you shall hear in your life."

Romulus looked down at her, blinking, confused, trying to process what she was saying—and a second too late, he noticed something in her hand, gleaming the sun. It was a dagger, shining gold, the thinnest, sharpest dagger he'd ever seen, and with lightning speed, Volusia drew it from her belt, spun around completely, and sliced his throat so fast, so sharply, he barely felt it happen.

Romulus, in shock, looked down and watched his own blood splatter down his chest, steaming hot, across the stone, collecting in a pool at his feet. He looked up and saw Volusia standing there, facing him calmly, emotionless, as if nothing had just happened. Her dark, evil eyes burned into his soul, as he raised his hand to his throat to try to stop the blood.

But it was too little, too late. It flowed across his hands, across his body, and he felt himself growing weak, dropping to his knees, staring up at her helplessly. He saw her black eyes staring down at him, knowing his life was ending, and he could not believe, of all things, that he had died here, in this place, that he had been killed at the hands of a girl, a young brazen girl, whose name, she was right, he would never forget. As his skull smashed down into the stone, it was her name, ringing in his ears, that was his final thought, a death knell, escorting him to hell.

*Volusia.*
*Volusia.*
*Volusia.*

# CHAPTER TWENTY-NINE

Darius walked with a smile on his face, a buoyancy to his step as he hurried through the winding streets of his village, greeting the day, preparing for another day of labor.

"What are you so happy about?" asked Raj, walking beside him with a dozen other boys as they prepared for another day of backbreaking labor.

"Yeah, what's gotten into you?" asked Desmond.

Darius tried to hide his smile as he looked down and did not say anything. These boys would not understand. He did not want to tell them about his date with Loti, did not want to say that he had found the love of his life, the girl he intended to marry, a girl who affected him like no other. He did not want to share with them that he felt he now had something to look forward to, that the blow of the Empire no longer bothered him as much. Because Darius knew that when he got the day off, she would be there, waiting for him; they had planned to rendezvous again that night, and he could think of nothing else.

Last night had been magical; Loti had blown him away with her pride and dignity—and most of all, her love for life. She had a way about her of rising above it all: it was as if she were not a slave, as if she did not lead a life of hardship. It inspired Darius, had made him realize he could change his life, could change his surroundings, just by perceiving it differently.

But Darius held his tongue; his friends would not understand.

"Nothing," Darius said. "It's nothing at all."

The group of them were about to turn down the road for the hills, when there came a sudden wail, a cry of grief, coming from the village center; he and the other boys turned and looked. There was something about that wail that caught Darius's attention, something that compelled him to turn and investigate.

"Where are you going?" Raj asked him. "We will be late."

Darius ignored him, following his instinct, and saw all the members of his village filtering toward the town center, and he joined them.

Darius made his way to the open clearing and saw sitting before the well, a woman whom he was shocked to recognize.

It was Loti's mother. She knelt there, rocking back and forth, eyes closed, weeping, alternately holding her palms up to the sky and laying them on her thighs as she bowed her head low, a woman in agony. A woman in grief.

The people crowded in, the town elders eventually circled around her, and Darius brushed past them, making his way to the front, his heart pounding in alarm, wondering what could have brought her here to this place. Wondering what could have happened.

Salmak, the leader of the elders stepped forward and raised his arms, and everyone fell silent as he faced her.

"My good woman," he said, "share with us your grief."

"The Empire," she said, between sobs. "They have taken my daughter from me!"

Darius felt his skin grow cold at her words, and he dropped his tools, feeling his palms tingling, wondering if he had heard her correctly.

Darius rushed forward, bursting into the circle, gaping at her.

"Speak again!" Darius said, his voice barely a whisper.

She looked up and glared at him, her dark eyes glistening with hate.

"They took her away," she said. "This morning. The taskmaster. The one who struck her. He decided to make her his, to take her as a wife. He has claimed the right of marriage. She is gone! Gone from me forever!"

Darius felt himself shaking inside, as he felt a tremendous rage rise up, a helplessness, an anger against the world. He felt something within him so violent he could barely control it.

"Who among you?" the woman shrieked, turning to all the village. "Who among you will rescue my daughter?"

All the brave warriors, all the men, all the elders, one by one, lowered their heads, looking away.

"Not one of you," she said softly, her voice filled with venom.

Darius, trembling with a sense of destiny, found himself stepping forward, into the center of the clearing, standing before Loti's mother, facing her.

He stood there, fists clenched, and felt his fate rising up within him.

"I shall go," he said, meeting her eyes. "I shall go alone."

She looked at him, her eyes cold, hard, and then finally she nodded back with a look of respect. Her look was one of obligation, one that bound them together forever.

"I will bring her back," Darius added, "or I will die trying."

With those words, Darius turned and marched through the village, the crowd parting for him, knowing exactly where he needed to go.

Darius twisted and turned until he found the small cottage, the one he had been to just the day before, and knocked three times as the man had instructed.

Soon, the door opened, and the small man inside looked out at him, eyes wide with intent and understanding. He beckoned him in.

Darius hurried inside and looked all about the cottage. It was like a large workshop, a fire raging in the fireplace on one side, and before it, a bench, on top of which he saw a blacksmith's tools.

And all around him, weapons. Weapons of iron. Weapons of steel. Weapons unlike any he had ever seen. Being caught possessing any one of these, Darius knew, would get him killed. Would get the entire village killed.

Darius reached out and laid his palms on the hilt of the finest sword he had ever seen. Its hilt was emerald green, and its blade had an emerald green tint to it as he turned it. He held it up high against the glowing light.

"Take it," the man said. "It is meant for you."

Darius examined it, and he saw in it his reflection. He no longer saw the face of a boy looking back, a boy playing with practice weapons, but the face of a hardened man. A man already morphed by suffering; a man seeking revenge. A man who was ready to become a true warrior. A man who was no longer a slave.

A man about to become free.

# CHAPTER THIRTY

Gwen lay nearly lifeless on the deck of the ship, her body feeling so heavy, barely stirring as a rat crawled over her wrist. She opened her eyes, so heavy, not having the energy to brush it off. She felt herself burning with fever, every muscle in her body aching, on fire. She saw that she was lying face-first on the wooden plank, her ear to the wood, the hollow sound below echoing in her head of the ocean lapping against the ship.

The early morning sun spread out over them like a blanket, and as she lay there, she opened her eyes just enough to see all the bodies sprawled out on the ship. She saw hundreds of her people, none of the moving, either too weak to move—or, she hated to think it, already dead. She thought of the baby, somewhere with Illepra, and prayed she was still alive.

Gwen slipped in and out of consciousness, the gentle rocking motion of the ocean keeping her awake. A flapping noise pervaded her dreams, and Gwen looked up, squinting, to see the mast, high up, a lone sail, flapping in the wind. The ship was drifting aimlessly at sea, no one manning it, at the mercy of a random breeze and wherever the ocean tides should take them.

Gwen had never felt more exhausted, not even when she'd been pregnant with Guwayne. She felt as if she had lived too many lifetimes, and a part of her felt that it did not have the strength to go on. A part of her felt as if she had already lived far longer than she was supposed to, and she did not know how she could muster the strength to keep going, to start all over again, even if they ever found the Empire. Especially without Thor, without her baby, and with all her people in such a state. If they were even alive.

Gwen let her head drop back down to the deck, it feeling too heavy, ready to give in. She tried to keep her eyes open, but she could not.

*Thor*, she thought. *I love you. If you find our son, raise him well. Raise him to remember me. To dream of me. Tell him how much I loved him.*

Gwen slipped out of consciousness for she did not know how long, until she was awakened by a distant noise, from high above. It was a lone screech, high up in the clouds, sounding so distant Gwen did not even know if she had really heard it.

The screech came again, insistent, and she dimly recognized it as that of an animal she knew from somewhere in her life. It sounded as if it were trying to rouse her.

It invaded her consciousness, refusing to let her sleep, to slip away—until finally, Gwen opened her eyes, recognizing it.

Estopheles.

Thor's falcon screeched incessantly, then swooped down, until Gwen felt it grazing her hair. Gwen lifted her head, brushed the rat off her hand, and with all her strength, she pushed hard, and got herself up to one knee.

Gwen rose, struggling, on shaky legs, and grabbed the rail on the side of the ship; with all her might, she pulled herself up, just enough to see over the rail.

There, laid out before her, was a sight she would never forget. Lying before her, filling the horizon, was land. It was a land unlike any she had ever seen, a city perched on the ocean, and in its center, shrouded in mist, two enormous stone pillars rising hundreds of feet into the sky, heralding a great city, a city of shining gold, sparkling in the sun like the entrance to heaven.

The ocean here was a foaming, fluorescent red, and it crashed against the shore, its glowing foam shooting up into the air, a shoreline of infinite variety, with endless contours and terrains, making the Ring seem minuscule. The two suns were huge in this sky, and beneath them, the red glow hung over everything, making it look like a land of fire.

Gwen took one final look at it, enthralled, and then she reeled, dizzy from hunger, burning from fever, and crashed onto the deck. She lay there, feeling the tides pulling them in.

If they lived, soon, they would be there.

The Empire.

Dead or alive, they had made it.

# CHAPTER THIRTY-ONE

Thor sprinted, charging up the mountaintop, keeping his eyes fixed on those tribesmen in the distance, winding their way up the volcano and carrying his son. Thor gasped as he ran, his brothers right behind him, his son in his sights, so close, hardly a few hundred yards away, determined to reach him or to die trying.

The entourage of tribesmen bore his son over their heads, on poles, in a small bassinet, bobbing up and down as they hiked. Thor saw the smoldering volcano, and he knew they were taking Guwayne to it, to sacrifice him.

Thor's heart was breaking inside as he urged his legs to go faster. He felt every muscle, every fiber of his being, about to explode; what he would give now for Mycoples.

Thor knew he had to do something.

"GUWAYNE!" he shrieked.

The group of tribesmen turned and saw Thor, and their eyes opened wide in panic. Thor did not wait, but hurled the spear in his hand with all his might, sending it flying fifty yards up the steep mountain slope, and watching with satisfaction as it pierced one of the tribesmen carrying his son in the back. The man screamed and collapsed.

The rest of the tribesmen, though, picked up the slack, and they took off at a jog, running Guwayne higher up the mountaintop. Thor chased after them, but he had no other spears to throw.

"GUWAYNE!" Thor shouted again, his voice echoing off the mountains.

Thor ran and ran, and he realized that he was gaining on them, able to move faster than the tribesmen. He was but seventy yards away…sixty…fifty. Thor ran faster, encourage, feeling confident that he could reach them in time. He would kill each and every one of them, rescue his boy, and bring him back to Gwendolyn.

Barely thirty yards away, Thor was getting close enough to see the panicked men's expressions. They were no match for Thor's speed, the speed of a man with his entire life on the line. He ran like a man possessed, more determined than he'd been for anything in his life.

Thor ran up the narrow mountain pass, narrowing, right on the edge of the cliff, running with everything that he had. They were hardly ten yards away now, just close enough for him to begin to draw his sword, to leap into the air, to butcher them. Thor reached down for the hilt of his sword—

And that was when it happened.

Suddenly, Thor felt an odd sensation beneath his feet, and he felt himself unsteady. Thor looked down and watched, in horror, as the path started to collapse.

Before Thor could react, the road gave way, caught up in a landslide, a giant avalanche. Thor found himself slipping, then falling, straight down the steep downslide, the mountain turning to mud, softened by the rains. He slid uncontrollably, down the mud, faster and faster, down hundreds of feet, shrieking, all his brothers sliding with him.

Thor spun around as he fell, looked up, and he saw his boy, so far away from him now, getting farther with each passing second.

"GUWAYNE!" Thor shrieked.

His shriek echoed off the mountains, again and again, the scream of a father losing a son, of a man losing everything he'd had.

*

Guwayne felt himself bouncing as the tribesmen carried him to the top of the volcano. He squinted his eyes at the thick smoke, finding it hard to breathe. His bassinet was hot, and he cried and cried, wanting to go down.

Guwayne heard a distant shriek, echoing off the mountains, and he recognized the voice. It was the sound of his father.

Guwayne wanted to be with him, wanted to be where he was. But the shriek faded, echoing away, and Guwayne knew that he was, once again, alone in the universe, left only with these strange men who looked down at him with hate.

Guwayne soon felt his bassinet lowered, and he looked over the edge and saw beneath him an endless flaming pit down into the earth. The heat was so intense here, the smoke rising up, and as the men set him down, he saw one of the men remove something shiny from his belt. It was sharp, and it glistened as he held it high, clutching it in his hand.

Guwayne screamed. He did not know what it was, but he knew that it was meant for him.

He screamed a scream to match his father's, and it echoed off the mountain range, bouncing back to him, a scream that he knew would go unanswered.

*

On a lonely beach at the edge of the Land of the Druids, there came a slight tremor in the ground. The tremor grew and grew, as the waves receded, and the sands bristled, and the chirping of birds and the calls of beasts quieted. Something amazing was happening, even for here, in the Land of the Druids, something that happened only once in centuries.

There was a sole object on this beach, one that remained here after Thorgrin and Mycoples had left, an object that was sitting there, alone, waiting.

As the morning sun shone down on it, there came a slight crack in the single dragon egg. The little dragon within it reached up and pushed against the shell, and the shell cracked again.

And again.

In moments, the perfectly still and silent air was breached by a single sound—a long, sharp cry. It was the cry of a new life coming onto the planet.

A dragon emerged, smashing the egg, rearing its head, spreading its wings, as the egg shattered to pieces all around it, sprinkling down onto the sand.

The dragon leaned back and arched its neck, and looked to the skies. The world was new. Everything was new. He did not understand it at all.

But he knew, deep down, that it was his. This world was his. All his. That nothing on this planet was stronger than he.

The dragon threw back its head and screeched, a high-pitched noise, soft at first, but growing louder by the second. Soon, he knew, it would be strong enough to destroy the world.

**COMING SOON!**

**BOOK #13 IN THE SORCERER'S RING**

Please visit Morgan's site, where you can join the mailing list, receive a free book, listen to audio, receive a free APP, hear exclusive news, see additional images, and find links to stay in touch with Morgan on Facebook, Twitter, Goodreads and elsewhere!

www.morganricebooks.com

**Books by Morgan Rice**

THE SORCERER'S RING
A QUEST OF HEROES
A MARCH OF KINGS
A FEAST OF DRAGONS
A CLASH OF HONOR
A VOW OF GLORY
A CHARGE OF VALOR
A RITE OF SWORDS
A GRANT OF ARMS
A SKY OF SPELLS
A SEA OF SHIELDS
A REIGN OF STEEL
A LAND OF FIRE

THE SURVIVAL TRILOGY
ARENA ONE (Book #1)
ARENA TWO (Book #2)

the Vampire Journals
turned (book #1)
loved (book #2)
betrayed (book #3)
destined (book #4)
desired (book #5)
betrothed (book #6)
vowed (book #7)
found (book #8)
resurrected (book #9)
craved (book #10)